Kappatoo

Other titles available in Armada

Barmy Jeffers and the Quasimodo Walk
Return of Barmy Jeffers and the Quasimodo Walk
Barmy Jeffers and the Shrinking Potion
J. H. Brennan

Adventures on the Santa Lucia series
Secret Persuader
Bomb Alert
Pamela Oldfield

Kappatoo 2: A Stitch in Time
Ben Steed

Black Harvest
The Beggar's Curse
The Witch of Lagg
Ann Pilling

Kappatoo

Ben Steed

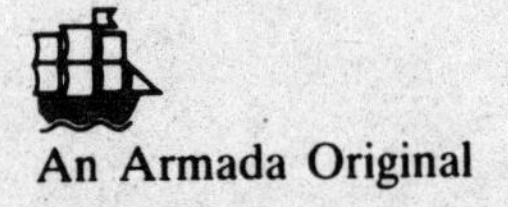

An Armada Original

For my wife

First published in Armada 1989

Armada is an imprint of the Children's Division,
part of the Collins Publishing Group,
8 Grafton Street, London W1X 3LA

Chapter One

When Simon Cashmere came home from the park his mother said: "Who are you?"

He blinked and thought about it. There were about four billion people in the world who didn't know who he was and it had never occurred to him that his mother might be one of them. If *she* didn't know who he was then his ambition to become a famous footballer wasn't going too well. You couldn't really be a famous *any*thing if your own mother didn't know who you were.

"Eh?" he asked, hoping to get the point cleared up before it had a serious effect on his self-esteem.

"What are you doing in my kitchen?" she went on, scowling at him.

"I live here," Simon protested.

"I don't think you do," she said with a scoffing sort of laugh. "I'm pretty sure nobody in this house would be *stupid* enough to play out in the park in the pitch dark!"

Oh, so that's what it was, Simon thought. Sarcasm. His mother was very good at being sarcastic. If they gave Nobel Prizes for Sarcasm she'd win it year after year. She wore sarcasm like other mothers wore aprons.

"It's not pitch dark—" he began, but she cut him short with an explosive screech which made the glasses rattle in the cupboard and sent the cat hurtling through his own special flap in the kitchen door. It was all right for the cat. He could just vanish when things got nasty. If Simon dived through the cat-flap every time his mother screeched she would knock him into the middle of next week. Leastways, that's what she was always saying she would do. Sometimes Simon wished he *was* in the middle of next week. Specially when the week he was in wasn't going too well. And anyway, he was too big to go through the cat-flap.

"Well, it jolly soon will be pitch dark!" said the Screech. "Don't they teach you *any*thing at school? Don't they tell you it's *dangerous* for children to be wandering about when it's dark?"

"But it's not dark . . ." Simon protested and went on: "Look, there's the sun. That big bright thing hiding behind the tree next door. They call it the Sun. It shines when it's not dark. See?" Sarcasm was something parents passed on to their kids. Parents, it seemed, weren't so good at taking it as they were at dishing it out.

"Don't you answer me back!" Mum yelled. "If I say it's dark, it's dark. How many times have I told you, eh? There're some funny people out there. I don't want you coming home all murdered . . . and just look at the state of you! You get into that bath pretty sharpish, my lad, and don't think you're watching football on telly tonight, 'cos you're not!"

Simon groaned. There was only one thing better than watching football on telly and that was actually playing it for Basingstoke Juniors. This row was just an excuse so his mum could watch some crummy soap opera. She was always watching crummy soap operas. She was even beginning to speak with an Australian accent.

"Oh, Mum . . ." he whined.

"You can do some revising. You've got an important test tomorrow."

"It's only Computer Studies," Simon pleaded. "And I'll never pass it anyway. It's just a waste of time."

"I'll be the judge of that."

Grovelling to Mother was a waste of time, too.

"Well, don't just stand there," she said.

"Bath! I'm not going to change my mind."

An hour later, Simon was sitting in his bedroom staring dumbly at a computer monitor. His father was standing beside his chair waiting for him to do something spectacular, like press one of the things on the keyboard. There were exactly eighty-three things he could press and none of them meant anything at all to him so the odds were stacked against him pressing the right one by accident.

"Well?" said Dad expectantly. Dad knew all about computers because he was a boffin. Some boys had fathers who played football in the park, but Simon got the boffin. Actually, Dad was all right. He wasn't anywhere near as bossy as Mum, but that was only because he was absent-minded. Boffins were supposed to be absent-minded. Only the previous evening, when Mum had been nagging Simon, she had turned to Dad and said "Talk to your son!" And Dad had looked up from his paper and asked: "What shall we talk about then, Simon?" in a really chatty sort of voice. It wasn't quite what Mum had in mind and she went berserk and frightened the cat. She was always frightening the cat. It was the only cat in Basingstoke that needed psychiatric counselling.

"It's no good, Dad," Simon said. "I'll never get the hang of these things."

"There's nothing to it," Dad said. "A subroutine's like delivering the papers. You go along Station Hill and when you come to number thirty you go up the path, deliver your paper, then come back to the road again." Dad had a way of explaining things which confused Simon even more. One minute he was doing Computer Studies, then next moment he was delivering newspapers.

"They don't have one at number thirty," he said.

"So we'll make the line number twenty-eight," his father told him as if it might help. Simon looked blank and just then his mother came in.

"Oh, I see!" she said to Dad. "Doing his homework *for* him now, are we? Why don't you just take the exam and make it *really* easy?"

Dad looked flustered. "I was only—"

"Well, don't!" Mother said. "Your dinner's on the table." She turned to Simon. "You just get on and do that yourself."

Simon persevered with the computer for another ten minutes or so and then programmed in a video-game called "Slug", where men chased nippy little slugs round a garden with bags of salt. It was about as interesting as watching one of Mum's crummy soap-operas, but a lot better than Computer Studies. He had managed to kill three slugs when the most momentous Event of his whole life happened.

Over the years, children who live in Basingstoke have learned not to expect momentous Events, or any sort of events, come to that. Events are what they read about in the papers when dawdling through a delivery round. Events are what happen to other people. So to have an Event happening in his bedroom – and not just any old event but a *momentous* Event – came as something of a surprise to Simon Cashmere. There was a sudden whooshing sound, a strangled cry and a thud – and that was it. Startled, Simon looked round his bedroom – but there was nothing out of the ordinary, or even out of place. Then the voice came from above and behind him.

"Innit marvellous!"

There, squashed between the top of his wardrobe and the ceiling, sat a boy – except he wasn't like any boy Simon had ever seen before, or wanted to see again. For a start he was wearing a kind of shiny green leotard which would have looked better on a girl. And then he had on a sort of skull cap with little bendy feelers poking out of the top like radar antennae and a big wrist-band with more buttons on it than Simon's computer. He would have looked ridiculous anywhere, never mind on top of a wardrobe, but Simon was too scared to say so or, indeed, to say anything at all. He just sat and gaped.

"That's what comes of people building new houses on top of the rubble of the old ones," the boy was saying as he tried to get down to floor level without laddering his tights. "You work out all the sums, get all the co-ordinates right – and crash bang wallop, the world's grown two metres! You wouldn't believe it, would you?" He finally fell most of the way to the floor and picked himself up grinning.

"Still," he went on. "It could've been worse. I could have gone the other way and ended up in the sludge under your basement." He frowned suddenly. "What's up? You look sick."

"Who . . . who are you?" Simon stammered.

"Oh, just some distant relative, I expect," the boy replied dismissively. "Kappa two seven zero nine three four. My mates call me Kappatoo. Maybe you're an ancestor."

As he spoke, Kappatoo wandered round the bedroom, touching things and screwing his nose up at them. He finally came to one of Simon's football boots and held it up between his finger and thumb.

"Ugh," he said. "What's this? What have you been treading in?"

"Mud," Simon told him.

"How disgusting." He dropped the boot and went on more briskly. "Anyway, you," he said. "We've gotta get organized. Loads to do, loads to explain—" He broke off to pick up Simon's football shorts.

"Poo-wee, hideous! Is everyone like this here? – or just you?"

Simon looked at him. He was beginning to feel guilty, having a stranger wandering round his bedroom criticizing his football gear. He was aware that there was something strangely familiar about the boy's face – as if he'd seen him somewhere before, but couldn't quite remember where. "What do you want?" he asked.

"Oh, right, yes," said Kappatoo. "The business in hand. We're gonna swap places, okay? No argument. Just slap on the time-belt, zap on down to two two seven zero, run a few rings round Sigmasix on the Droid Eliminator then boogie on back to the present. In the meantime I'll do your Computer Studies test, knock out a sinchy hundred percent and whackado-chicky, we're both flavour of the month. Got it?"

Simon swallowed hard. "Two two seven zero?" he echoed.

"A.D. That's two hundred and eighty-three years from now. I wouldn't send you back to two hundred and eighty B.C. now, would I? They probably still had dinosaurs knocking about the place then." The thought seemed to amuse him.

"You're from the future?" Simon asked, disbelieving. Kappatoo raised his eyes to the ceiling. "Are you thick or something?" he asked. "Or do you just pretend?"

Simon wanted to be sure. "You're from the future and you want to swap places with me?"

"Yup! Just for the day. Smooth idea, huh?"

"It's impossible," Simon protested.

"*Now* it is. In *your* time. But it's not impossible in *my* time. Look, dummy, a hundred years ago they didn't even have television, right? *That* was impossible. They couldn't even fly!" He suddenly seemed to remember when he was. "Oh, you still can't, can you," he added apologetically.

"Can *you* fly?" Simon asked.

"'Course I can!" Kappatoo pressed a button on his wrist-band and floated up a foot or so from the floor. "Nothing to it," he shrugged. It looked funny, seeing him shrug while dangling in space. Simon looked round suspiciously for wires, but there weren't any. Kappatoo dropped back to the floor. "Look, we gotta get a move on," he said urgently. "We gotta change clothes. I gotta tell you where everything is—"

"But you've got a funny head," Simon protested. Kappatoo looked indignant. "Have you seen *yours* lately?" he protested, and then realized what Simon was looking at.

"Oh, this," he said. "It's not my head. It does come off, you know." He pulled off the skull cap and Simon immediately understood why he looked so familiar. The boy's face was exactly the same as the one Simon saw in the mirror every morning.

"It's an Ambience Optimizer," Kappatoo said. "We all wear them."

"Why?" Simon asked.

"For clever scientific reasons. Are you going to get your gear off or not?"

Simon looked puzzled and didn't move. Kappatoo sighed and decided to try another tack.

"Okay, look, you're not getting anywhere with Tracey Cotton, right?" He couldn't have said anything more startling. Tracey Cotton was in Simon's class at school and he was madly in love with her. Well, he was madly in love with football, really, but Tracey came a close second. What was startling was the fact that nobody knew about it – except Tracey, of course, because he was always telling her.

"What do you know about Tracey?" Simon asked.

"Not a lot. I just came across her in a history lesson. That's where I found you."

"We're in the history books?"

"Not books exactly . . ."

"You mean I'm going to be famous?" Simon said excitedly. Kappatoo looked at him disdainfully. "Shouldn't think so," he said. "I wouldn't know."

"But you did us in history!"

"We didn't *do* you in history," Kappatoo sneered. "You *are* history. *Every*one gets to be history eventually. History's boring."

The possibilities began to dawn on Simon. "Did you see what happens to me?" he asked. "Like with Tracey and stuff like that?"

Kappatoo grimaced. "Never gave it a thought. Could have looked it up, I guess. You can check all that stuff out for yourself."

"You mean I'll be able to look into my own future?"

"No sweat. Except it'll be history then."

It was all very confusing to Simon, but Kappatoo seemed to accept it all as perfectly normal. "I'll tell you what, though," he was saying. "You won't get anywhere at all with Tracey unless you brighten up your act a bit. She wants style, flair, a cool line in chat. She doesn't want to know about football and that's all you ever talk about. If you like, I'll throw that in as well. All part of the package. I'll smooth-talk her so's when you come back she'll be crazy about you, okay?"

Simon was beginning to waver. Unconsciously he unfastened the buttons of his shirt. "And what's this Sigmasix?" he asked. "And the Droid what-didja-call-it?"

"Eliminator. It's a sport. Like a cross between a video-game and being tortured slowly by a robot. Sigmasix is a creep who thinks he's good at it. In fact you can do me a favour when you get there and give him a good hiding."

Simon peeled off his shirt. "Are you sure this is going to work?"

"Do pigs fly?" Kappatoo asked.

"No."

"Ah, not yet they don't," Kappatoo said and handed over the Ambience Optimizer. "Here, try this for size."

Chapter Two

The twenty-third century, where Kappatoo lived, was super-advanced and pretty amazing. Trouble was, science had done away with diseases and people didn't die unless they got hit by a bus, and since there weren't any buses any more, that wasn't very often. In fact it was never. So people only died when they got really, *really* old and fell to bits. There were people everywhere. Even more people than there were fleas on Simon's cat. It was hardly surprising that they didn't have enough names to go round – that's why Kappatoo's proper name was Kappa/270934. There were nearly half a million Kappas living in Basingstoke alone, never mind the rest of the country. And the reason they didn't have any buses was because there wasn't anywhere people could go without falling over millions of other people – unless it was somewhere far out like the Moon or Pluto. So people in the future were extremely lazy.

Everything they wanted and needed came to their houses – or "Domes", as they were called. Machines did all the work and computers did all the thinking, and Future People just lazed about all day pressing buttons and eating and generally getting pretty bored.

When Simon Cashmere woke up in the twenty-third century he thought somebody had switched out all the lights and thrown him in a car-wash. Big, soft brushes were swirling round and over his body, and it was all warm and wet. It was only when they stopped, and a hot blast of air dried him out, that he remembered Kappatoo and the deal he had made with him. After hours of detailed explanations about what he could expect, Simon fastened on the time-belt and pressed a button. It was a peculiar feeling, flying forward two hundred and eighty years – rather like going round in a tumble dryer – not that Simon had ever done it, but that cat had, once, by mistake, and hadn't been too impressed. Fortunately the experience didn't last long. There was a big bump and he found himself in Kappatoo's bedroom . . . Simon, that is. Not the cat.

It was a strange room. Loads of shiny surfaces and weird colours. There was a console in the middle of the floor like a monster version of Simon's own computer – and a bunk-like bed against one wall. That was it. No other furniture at all. Simon had shrugged to himself and plonked down on the bed. He'd intended to lie there and think about it, but that was all he could remember. Now he had woken up in a car-wash. It was very confusing.

After about two minutes – and Simon found it very difficult to know how long it was when his watch was two hundred and eighty years wrong – a cover slid back from over him and disappeared into the wall. Looking down at himself, Simon was surprised to find he was wearing the same shiny leotard he'd put on the evening before, but now it was red. There wasn't time to wonder how that had happened. Suddenly the bed itself bent in the middle and he was sitting up and having an Ambience Optimizer plonked on his head by an unseen robot arm. He was just thinking how amazing it was that Future People should be showered and washed before they'd even got up, when a small hatch opened in the wall beside him and a tray emerged with a beaker of fruit juice on it. He picked it up and immediately a tinny sort of computer-voice asked: "What would you like for breakfast?"

Simon looked for where the Voice came from, but couldn't see anything. He shrugged and thought greedy.

"Bacon, eggs, mushrooms, tomatoes, two slices of fried bread and a sausage." Try *that* for size, he thought, and added as an afterthought: "Oh, and turn the eggs over, please. I don't like them all soggy in the middle." There was silence for a moment. Simon imagined the Computer was thinking about it, but it wasn't.

"Please return your beaker to the tray," it stated.

Simon drank the contents and obeyed. The tray slid neatly back into the wall and the door closed. It opened again immediately with a plate full of strangely-coloured cubes. It certainly didn't look like breakfast as Simon knew it. "I asked for bacon and eggs and stuff," he complained.

"That's what you've got," the Computer-Voice told him in a crowing sort of tone. Apparently computers in the twenty-third century had learned to be cheeky.

Simon picked up one of the cubes and sniffed it. It had an eggy sort of smell in spite of being bright green, and then he was aware of other smells – frying bacon and tomatoes . . . all the things he'd asked for in fact. He began to chomp his way into it and discovered it tasted exactly like the food he was used to only more so. He enjoyed it so much he even thought about putting on the time-belt, whisking back ten minutes and scoffing it all over again – but that would have meant another spell in the tumble dryer and he didn't think he could cope with that on a full stomach.

"Is there anything else you require?" asked the Computer-Voice. Simon gave it some thought and considered asking for an ice cream, but that would probably have come out as a green cube as well.

"No," he said finally.

The tray slid away and returned immediately with a round ball which looked a bit like a gob-stopper.

"I said no," Simon told the Computer.

"I heard you," the Computer told Simon.

"So what's that then?"

"It's for cleaning your teeth with." It was the strangest toothbrush Simon had ever seen.

"What do I do with it?" he asked.

"Where are your teeth?" the Computer asked back.

"In my mouth," said Simon.

"Then you wouldn't expect to push the teeth-cleaner up your nose, would you?"

Simon blinked. Even computers were sarcastic. This one seemed every bit as sarcastic as Simon's mother. He popped the little ball into his mouth. It was all squashy like a marshmallow, but it didn't behave like one. It rolled all round his teeth of its own accord, fizzing as it went – and then the tray popped back and out again with an empty beaker.

"Please spit the teeth-cleaner into the beaker," the Computer said. Its voice sounded weary, as if it were bored with the morning's proceedings. Simon did as he was told and the tray and beaker vanished.

"Now what?" Simon asked, but the Computer didn't reply. "Are you still there?" he continued, feeling lonely all of a sudden.

"Of course."

"So why didn't you answer?"

" 'Now what?' isn't a complete question."

Simon sighed. "What do I do now?"

"What you choose to do is of no interest or concern to me. I am a Master-Class Domestic Computer. My function is to provide information and services." The Computer's tone was that of a snooty waiter in a posh restaurant.

"Sorry I asked," said Simon, feeling as though he'd been caught shovelling peas down with his soup spoon.

"However," Computer went on, "if you require advice, I suggest you familiarize yourself with your surroundings and try to look as if you belong here." Simon's eyes widened in surprise. He didn't widen them deliberately to see anything better, they just did it on their own for no particular reason.

"You . . . you know who I am?" he asked.

"You are Simon Cashmere."

Simon's panic began to rise. "Who else knows?"

"In your own time, sixty-two people know you to be Simon Cashmere." It wasn't what he meant, but the answer jolted him.

"Sixty-two? Is that all?"

"By comparison, it is less than those who know Mikhail Gorbachov, President of the Soviet Union, who was extremely famous, and Ndinko Mbusi who wasn't famous at all."

"Who's he?"

"A small boy abandoned by his parents to fend for himself in the African jungle."

"How many people know him?"

"None. He was known personally by only five warm-blooded creatures. Four were friendly monkeys and one a hostile water buffalo. This figure does not include the lion which ate him without being formally introduced."

"He was eaten by a lion? That's awful!" Simon was horrified. Perhaps he shouldn't moan about only sixty-two people knowing him. In fact he shouldn't moan about anything at all if some poor kids were being abandoned and eaten by lions and stuff like that. At least he was looked after. And he *would* be famous one day – when everyone realized what a brilliant footballer he was. "How about now?" he asked. "In this time? How many people know I'm Simon Cashmere?"

"None."

"So how come you do?"

"I was required to locate you in history, calculate the spacial and temporal co-ordinates and effect the Time Transfer."

"Oh." It didn't mean anything to Simon, but that was his fault for asking. Perhaps the Computer was right. Maybe he should stop chatting and make a start on getting to know the place.

He looked round the room and decided to investigate the console in the middle of the floor first. But just then, before he had a chance to investigate anything at all, another Momentous Event happened. It wasn't quite as spectacular as the arrival of Kappatoo had been, but it was still pretty startling. It was the arrival of Kappatoo's father.

He was extremely tall, extremely thin, and

running on the spot. If that wasn't bad enough, he was dressed in tight, shiny shorts and vest and had an Ambience Optimizer on his head. The whole effect was rather silly, but then Simon had to admit that he probably didn't look too clever himself. And anyway, he was much too worried to laugh. What if Father realized that his son wasn't really his son? How could he explain things to him? Suddenly the whole idea of the Swap seemed doomed to failure before it had even begun. But Father wasn't even looking at him.

"Good, good, good," he was saying, still running on the spot. He was lifting his knees so high they were nearly prodding him on the chin. "Glad to see you're up. Lots of exercises to do. We'll start with press-ups. Me first, then you." And with that, he fell down onto the floor and began to heave himself up and down on his arms.

Simon looked astonished. Simon *was* astonished. What sort of fatherly behaviour was this? And to make matters even more ridiculous, Father couldn't even *do* press-ups. Not properly. Not like Simon did them on training nights for Basingstoke Juniors. He was really straining and struggling and going bright red in the face – and when he got to six he collapsed with an exhausted but triumphant grin on his face.

"There," he beamed. "Six. Now see if you can do half as many!" Half as many! Simon could do *five* times as many. He crouched down on the floor, stretched himself out and began pressing up and down briskly. When he got to five, Father began clapping excitedly. When he got to ten, Father fell silent. When he got to twenty, Simon glanced over his shoulder to see Father leaning against the wall clutching his chest and staring in amazement. He stopped and stood up.

"Are you all right?" he asked.

"All right?" Kappatoo's father yelled. "All right? That was brilliant!" And suddenly he was dancing round Simon and hugging him.

"Twenty press-ups!" he was saying. "*Twenty*! I've never seen anything like it! You can do it. You can beat that snotty-nosed Sigmasix and all that snotty-nosed Sigma family! We'll show 'em. Just think! Kappatoo, Champion of the Droids!" Simon glowed with pleasure. Twenty press-ups was nothing – and here was Kappatoo's father thinking it was brilliant! Future People must be really weedy, he decided. Why even his own father could do press-ups, and he was a boffin. Boffins weren't supposed to do anything but boff. He shrugged modestly and Kappatoo's father beamed with delight again and clapped him on the back.

"My son," he said proudly. "Champion of the Droids!"

If being a champion is this easy, thought Simon, living in the future could be fun . . .

Chapter Three

Kappatoo must have spent at least a quarter of an hour lying awake in Simon's bed wondering why he wasn't being washed and dressed. He passed another weary ten minutes or so waiting for his breakfast to appear through a hole in the wall. Neither of these things happened. Then he remembered his history lessons. In the twentieth century, he recalled, mothers actually *cooked* breakfast themselves without any help at all from the computer and food processor. It was all very embarrassing to think about, but perhaps mothers washed and dressed you as well. He waited yet another ten minutes for Simon's mother to appear, but that didn't happen either. In fact only one thing happened. The cat came in.

Kappatoo had never seen a cat before. He'd seen something that *looked* like a cat, but that was an Alien on the planet Porex in the Andromeda Galaxy. He had been there on holiday with his family once and there were furry things lurking about wherever you looked. Kappatoo was used to Aliens from foreign planets. Some schools did exchange visits with them and for three weeks every summer Basingstoke was flooded out with creepy-crawlies from all over the universe. Most of them were hideously ugly – like the *Wurlops* from Alpha Pavonis which had two heads and six arms and cheated on the Droid Eliminator. And others, like the *Gluids* from Alula Borealis, which had really weird habits that didn't bear thinking about. And most of them were pretty dumb. You couldn't reason with them. It was only by a miracle of Earth science you could even talk to them.

Way back in the middle of the twenty-first century, a famous scientist had invented a cunning machine called a *Mindword*. This was a bit like a radio which tuned in to brain-waves and changed them into words. Nobody bothered learning languages any more, they just used a *Mindword* – and it was especially useful for talking to Aliens because some of them didn't even make sounds human ears could hear, but squeaked like dog whistles or made strange noises like elephants burping at the bottom of a big tub of treacle. Over the years the boffins had made the device smaller and smaller until it was just another gadget that Future People took for granted. Kappatoo, like everyone else, had one on his wrist-band. Not that he used it much. Only for three weeks during the summer and when his father decided to haul them off to far-out planets for their holidays. Right now the cat was looking at him curiously and wrinkling its nose in a very Porex-Alien kind of way. Kappatoo pressed the button on his *Mindword* and said: "Meiow".

Actually, the *Mindword* said "Meiow". Kappatoo merely thought "Hello".

The cat blinked again, surprised, and said "Hello" back. If humans wanted to talk cat-language the least it could do was be polite.

Kappatoo wondered what kind of Alien it was. "Meiow?" he asked.

"I'm a cat," replied the cat wearily. "What do you think I am, a stick of rhubarb?" The cat was nearly as sarcastic as Kappatoo's computer, but at least it wasn't as dumb as some of the Aliens. It seemed to know what was what, and right now Kappatoo needed some advice.

"Meiow meeiow, mewk?" he asked.

The cat frowned and put its head on one side. "How do *I* get a wash around here?" he repeated. "Me personally?"

"Meiow," Kappatoo agreed. The cat licked himself a few times. "Like that," he explained and Kappatoo felt sick. The twentieth century was even worse than he'd thought. Licking yourself wasn't a particularly scientific or sophisticated way of taking a wash. He shrugged, tried it anyway, and discovered that apart from tasting pretty nasty there were bits of himself he couldn't reach – like the back of his neck. "Meiook!" he complained.

The cat groaned in a martyred sort of voice and licked its paw. "You have to do this," he told Kappatoo, and rubbed the paw on the back of his head. "But that's if you're a cat. I think you'll find most humans use the bathroom." With that, it yawned, stretched, and jumped out the window, leaving Kappatoo to wonder what a bathroom was.

He didn't have to wonder for long. Simon's mother burst in, gripped him painfully by the hair and dragged him out of bed.

"Didn't you hear me calling you?" she screeched. Simon had warned him about the Screech. "I've been shouting and yelling for at least an hour. What have you been doing up here all this time?"

"Talking to the cat," Kappatoo told her and was smartly clipped on the back of his head for being cheeky. Actually he had been vaguely aware of someone calling. The trouble was they had been calling for Simon and Kappatoo hadn't bothered to listen. He made a mental note to remember who he was supposed to be in the future. Or, in the past – as he really was.

"Well, are you going to have a shower or not?" Simon's mother demanded, and with a sinking feeling in his stomach, Kappatoo suddenly remembered what bathrooms were all about. Showers were one of the weird habits the *Gluids* had brought from Alula Borealis. All the families that were stupid enough to do the exchange had to have shower rooms fitted in their Domes – and the *Gluids* didn't even dry themselves properly but paddled water everywhere and dripped. "Great Dripping Gluids!" had been a saying at school for months after they'd gone.

"Great Dripping Gluids!" said Kappatoo, thinking back on it, and Simon's mother tutted impatiently.

"Never mind all that," she said. "Just get yourself ready for school."

Twenty minutes later and a hundred times more disgruntled, Kappatoo stood in front of Simon's wardrobe mirror and wondered about the school tie. He couldn't remember what on earth he was supposed to do with it. He wished he'd paid more attention in history lessons. First he threaded it through the belt loops in his trousers, then he tucked it like a hanky in his jacket pocket, and finally he tied it in a bow over the top of his head. It still didn't look right, but it would have to do. He was already exhausted. Back home in the future the only time he left his room was at family dinner, once a week, and on the rare occasions when they took trips to other planets. All the rest of the time everything came to him. One word to the Central Computer and school appeared all around him – or the youth club, or the beach or the Droid Eliminator or whatever he wanted. Walking around simply wasn't done. So far today he had walked across the landing, showered, dried himself, brushed his teeth with some prehistoric tool with bristles in it, walked *back* from the bathroom and got himself dressed! And the worst was yet to come. He actually had to *walk* downstairs. Goodness only knew how he would climb back up them at the end of the day. All the exercise would probably kill him.

By the time he reached the kitchen door, Kappatoo was panting and perspiring. It was very important to look normal and Simon-like, though, so he stood there for a few minutes getting his breath back. Then he made his entrance.

"Hi folks, how's you all?"

The effort at being normal was wasted. Simon's dad didn't even look up from his *Boffins' Weekly* and Mum simply banged a bowl down on the table and poured into it what looked like a bunch of small, dead leaves. Then she turned busily back to a metal container that was whistling and blowing steam all over the kitchen. Only Lucy, Simon's kid sister, seemed to notice him properly. She sat staring at him for several seconds before deciding that he was only showing off by wearing his tie in a bow over his head and she wasn't going to encourage him even by saying how silly he looked. Kappatoo took his place at the table and examined the bowl of dead leaves. It seemed pretty obvious that he was supposed to eat them, so he cautiously popped one into his mouth. It was dry and crisp and tasteless. Lucy was looking at him even more curiously now but she still didn't say anything.

"Pen," said Dad, suddenly and surprisingly. He was still reading his paper but holding out his hand in a Kappatoo-ish direction. Mum spun round irritably.

"How many times have I told you – I

don't like you doing crosswords at the breakfast table!"

"No, dear," said Dad and turned back to Kappatoo. "Have you a pen?"

Mum tutted and looked at the ceiling. Kappatoo wondered what a pen was. Dad noticed the school tie and examined the arrangement with scientific curiosity. "Interesting," he declared. Then he saw a ballpoint protruding from Simon's jacket pocket and reached forward to borrow it.

"He's only showing off," said Lucy. "I expect he thinks it's trendy or something. *I* think he looks like a girl and not a very pretty one at that."

Mum glanced at Kappatoo and saw how he was dressed. "Oh yes, very clever," she said and bustled round the table towards him. "I'm sure Miss Tweedie will be really impressed, *but* . . ." She didn't say *but* what; she merely unfastened the tie and busily began knotting it properly round Kappatoo's neck. "Fourteen years old," she was saying, "and Mummy still has to dress you. Shall I feed you as well?" Kappatoo secretly wished she would. He was starving hungry and had no idea at all how to eat the dead leaves.

"There, that's better," she said, tucking down his shirt collar. "Now, just you get on with those cornflakes while I pour out the tea." Kappatoo looked blank. Perhaps this swap with Simon wasn't such a good idea after all. Lucy was now looking at him in a funny sort of way as if she knew something. Once again Simon's dad accidentally saved him.

"Measure of data transmission speed between serial communication devices. Four letters," he asked. He was talking to himself, really, because he didn't think anyone else in the household was clever enough to understand complicated scientific things, but it was easy stuff to Kappatoo. He had done it all along with nuclear bombs and other Basic Science when he was in the Infants.

"Baud," he said, and spelt it out. "B-A-U-D."

"Of course," said Dad, writing it into his crossword and thought no more about it. Then Lucy noticed Kappatoo's new wrist-band.

"You've got a new watch!" she said indignantly, and turned to her mother. "Why has Simon got a new watch and I haven't?"

"Don't be silly," Mum told her. "Of course he hasn't got a new watch. Let me see . . . !" Kappatoo glared at Lucy and held his arm up to Simon's mum.

"Where did you get that?" she demanded.

"Borrowed it from a friend," Kappatoo

answered quickly. A little lie now might save a lot of trouble later on.

"What friend?"

That was the trouble with lies. They always led to other lies until the whole thing got really messy.

"Delta Four," Kappatoo told her. He was the first of his school-mates that came to mind.

"Del?" Lucy repeated. "You haven't got any friends called Del."

"Just make sure you give it back to him," Mum said. "Now hurry up, or you'll miss the school bus."

While Kappatoo was finding life in the twentieth century something of a struggle, Simon Cashmere, two hundred and eighty-three years in the future, was really beginning to enjoy himself. Father had gone out excitedly, to tell Mother how many press-ups "Kappatoo" had done, and Simon was left alone to discover what the Future was all about. And it was brilliant! The console in the middle of his room looked very complicated, but Simon didn't even have to use it. He had only to speak and the computer worked everything out for itself. If he wanted anything he only had to ask for it and it came. But most astonishingly, if he wanted to go somewhere he didn't have to move. The place just appeared around him.

"I want to be at Wembley for the World Cup Final in the year 1966," he said – and he was there! Of course, he wasn't actually in Wembley and he didn't travel through time. It just *seemed* that way. The console dropped down into the floor and all four walls and the ceiling became giant hologram screens. It was just an illusion – but it was so real you could hear the crowd and even feel the sunshine and smell the onions on the hot-dog seller's tray! And to get back he had only to say the word "Dome" and Wembley disappeared and he was in Kappatoo's room. Simon was so excited that he did all sorts of things. He went big-game hunting in Africa, tobogganing in Canada and deep-sea fishing off the Great Barrier Reef – all without moving a yard! And then the phone rang.

At first, he didn't realize it was a phone. Apart from the fact that there wasn't a receiver as such, it sounded more like the cat calling its girlfriend at two o'clock in the morning.

"What's that noise?" he asked the Computer.

"It's the telephone," the Computer told him. "Somebody wants to talk to you."

Panic seized Simon. Not only didn't he know

anybody in the future, he didn't even know where the phone was.

"What do I do?" he asked.

"Try saying 'hello'," the Computer said. "It usually works."

Simon took a deep breath.

"Hello?" Immediately the walls became screens again – but this time he wasn't somewhere exotic or futuristic but in his own living room in the twentieth century. And there was Kappatoo in *his* school uniform, sitting on the floor with the telephone. Except it didn't look much like a telephone any more. Kappatoo had taken it to bits and added wires, aerials and things so it looked more like a model Simon had once made of HMS *Victory*.

"How did you do that?" Simon asked.

"Ah, great!" Kappatoo said. "It worked. Can you hear me?"

"Of course I can."

Kappatoo didn't even look at him, but went on talking into the phone. "Listen, I've got problems—"

"Why don't you look at me?" Simon asked.

"Because I can't *see* you, can I, dummy?"

"But I'm here! Right beside you!"

Kappatoo looked exasperated. "No, you're not, you're in my room in the twenty-third century. You haven't travelled through time, it just seems that way." Simon looked round his living room. It didn't *feel* like an illusion. Not until he went to sit on the sofa and fell through onto the floor. He stood up and tried to touch things, but his hands passed through them, even though he could *see* they were there.

"So how come you can't see me?" Simon asked. Kappatoo sighed wearily.

"Because you've got my computer in the twenty-third century. All I've got is this dumb telephone – and even that didn't work till I added a few bits to it. Do you understand?"

Simon nodded, but he didn't understand at all and Kappatoo didn't see him anyway, so nodding was a waste of time. "What do you want?" he asked.

Kappatoo stammered and stuttered and didn't know where to begin. Simon had got it so *easy* in the future because everything was done for him. Here in the twentieth century you had to do things for yourself, and some things were really difficult – like understanding cornflakes.

"I want to know how to eat cornflakes," he began. "Then I want to know what a school bus is and what I should aim at it with . . ."

"*Aim* at it?"

"Your mother said I wasn't to miss it. You only miss things when you don't aim at them properly."

Simon laughed. "The school bus is what takes you to school and you miss it by arriving after it's gone."

It was good to see Kappatoo looking totally confused.

"Where does it arrive at?"

"The end of the street."

"And how do I get there?"

"Walk. It's only a hundred metres or so."

Kappatoo's mouth dropped open in horror.

"A *hundred* metres?" Simon couldn't have shocked him more if he'd said a hundred miles. "I can't possibly walk that far!"

Future People really were weedy if they couldn't walk a little distance like that. "And what do you want to know about the cornflakes?" Simon asked.

"They taste horrible. Your sister said I should put milk on them. What's milk?"

"It's sort of white stuff. Comes out of a cow."

"A cow?"

"Big animal with horns," Simon explained. He added: "It goes moo," in case the extra information might help.

Kappatoo looked as if he were about to

be violently sick. "And you eat this stuff?"

"Well, drink it. It's really good for you."

Kappatoo obviously didn't believe him.

"I think I'll go hungry," he said. "Boy, you really do live like animals!"

This made Simon defensive and angry. "Look, it was your idea to swap," he said. "*I* never asked you to."

"You never told me you had to drink white stuff out of a cow!"

Simon was suddenly tired of arguing, and anyway there were all sorts of exciting things he still wanted to do in the future, but he didn't know how to hang up.

"Oh . . . Dome!" he said, remembering the magic word, and the illusion of his living room vanished. Kappatoo continued to moan for several more seconds before he realized that Simon wasn't there. He thought of dialling the future again, but there didn't seem any point. He hung up, and just then Lucy came running in.

"Mummy says you've got five minutes left before—" she began urgently, but stopped in horror when she saw what Kappatoo was doing. "Oo, you've broken the phone! You wait – I'm going to tell Daddy!" And with that she turned and ran out again.

Chapter Four

The one thing Kappatoo *didn't* need was Simon's sister rushing off, telling tales, and bringing back mums and dads and all kinds of hassle. He could just imagine it. Mum would be really stroppy because he'd "broken" the telephone – and Dad, being a boffin, would almost certainly be intrigued by all the clever future things he'd done to it. Then there would be questions. They would want to know who he was, where he'd come from and what he'd done with Simon. The whole story would come out and he would be sent back to the twenty-third century with his tail between his legs – not that he *had* a tail, of course. His real mother and father would be furious and so would the future-police because time-travel was strictly against the law, and snotty-nosed Sigmasix would be gloating because his rival had tried cheating on the Droid Eliminator and . . . and . . . and . . . "It doesn't bear thinking about," he thought with a shudder.

In fact he didn't really think about it, because there wasn't time. Before Lucy had taken two steps out of the room, Kappatoo had not only decided what to do, but put his plan into action.

When they invented time-travel towards the end of the twenty-first century, the scientists were so excited that they all went a little crazy trying to prove what new and amazing tricks they could do. It was mega-confusing for everybody. Nobody really knew whether they were coming or going, never mind what day of the week it was. And when time-travel became available to everyone the whole world was turned inside out and upside down. If schoolchildren made a mess of their exams, they would simply find out the answers then whoosh back in time and do the exams again. And others just couldn't wait to see that they had got for Christmas so they would whizz forward a few months to have a look. And their parents were no better. They would get up on Monday mornings ready to go to work, think: "Why should I?" and pop back to Friday afternoon so they could enjoy the weekend all over again. Life was all weekends, holidays and Christmas – and if that sounds like fun it wasn't really because nobody was actually doing all the horrible things that had to be done, like eating cabbage and putting the rubbish out. And with some people whizzing backwards and others whizzing forwards it became a whizzing-dizzy time in world history. So the governments all got together and said that anyone caught travelling through time would go to prison for a hundred years. Which was all very silly because the people who *did* get caught just whizzed forward a hundred years and it was like they had never been to prison at all. Or they would whizz back a couple of days and make sure they didn't get caught in the first place. So eventually all the time-belts were called in and nobody was allowed to keep one. Most of them were destroyed, but some were kept in museums to remind people, and just a few stray ones were overlooked and left in attics and garden sheds. Kappatoo found his in the spare room of his Dome in Basingstoke, buried under a load of junk.

But the scientists were not to be thwarted. If their invention was against the law they decided they would have to twist it round a little bit so that it *wasn't* against the law. If people weren't allowed to travel through Time, then they could always stay where they were and get Time to travel around *them*. In just the same way, if it was against the law to travel by train from

Basingstoke to Edinburgh, you could easily sit in the train at Basingstoke station and not go anywhere at all – just get somebody to push Edinburgh down the track instead. Well, of course, it wouldn't be all *that* easy, because first they would have to push the station out, then all the buildings and stuff, and fields of cows, and woods and London and the Midlands and York Minster and Hadrian's Wall – and lots of people would moan about being uprooted and shunted through Basingstoke anyway . . . specially the northern ones who like chip butties and Manchester United and all the northern things that you just can't get in Hampshire. Apart from which it would be Problem-City to find anyone with the energy to push half the country three hundred miles. But when you're sitting in a train it's easy to imagine that it isn't moving at all and that it's the stations and fields and everything else that's whooshing past . . .

. . . and that's how Kappatoo dealt with Lucy except he wasn't moving Edinburgh. He stayed exactly where he was but pressed the Fast-Rewind button on his wrist-band and rewound Time. It looked really funny. First of all Lucy ran backwards into the room, then she turned and said:

"Yddad llet ot gniog m'I – tiaw ouY . . ." and other strange things which sounded, not surprisingly, like a record being played back to front. Then she turned again and ran backwards out of the room. At this point, Kappatoo pressed the Time-Freeze button on his wristband and she stopped, motionless in the middle of a backwards stride with her mouth open while Kappatoo put the telephone back together again. When he had finished and the telephone had been returned to its table and all the wires had been cleared away, he pressed the Time-Restart button and everything was normal again. Lucy ran into the room as if none of this had happened and said:

"Mummy says you've got five minutes left before the bus goes, so you'd better hurry." Kappatoo smiled to himself. Future-Science could be useful when nobody else knew about it. Perhaps this little trip to the twentieth century would be fun after all . . .

The school Simon Cashmere went to was called Sir Rudyard Freebootle after a really famous Basingstoke person who was knighted by the Queen for inventing a new hamburger sauce. The sauce was so delicious that it sold to every country in the world except Togo in

West Africa where you couldn't get a decent hamburger anyway. This brought in loads of money from exports and made Sir Rudyard extremely rich and famous and worth naming a school after. Kappatoo knew all about this because he checked up on it in History. He also knew the names of his teachers, especially Miss Tweedie, and most of the boys and girls in Simon's class. Before deciding to make the Swap with Simon he had researched the subject very thoroughly. What he *hadn't* taken into account was the hundred-metre walk to catch the school bus.

Future People don't have to walk very far at all, partly because there's nowhere to go without falling over all the other people, and partly because science goes on inventing all kinds of devices to save people the trouble. Once upon a time, thousands of years ago, everyone had to walk *every*where. Then they invented the horse . . . well, they didn't invent it as such. Some caveman probably fell out of a tree onto one – and the horse, understandably surprised at this intrusion into its body-space, galloped off in a direction which just happened to be close to where all the caves were. And when he fell off the caveman thought:

"Ugh grunt ouch, ee by gum eckie thump."

– which was Prehistoric for "Gosh! That's a jolly good way of getting home from the tree," and after that everyone went round on horses. Then they invented the cart . . . and the train and the car and the aeroplane, the boat, bus, balloon and escalator. And by the time they got to the twenty-third century people had become so lazy it took a real effort just to walk across the room. When Kappatoo arrived, panting, at the garden gate – after a mighty trek of five metres from the front door – the end of the street seemed to be a mere dot on the far horizon. It would have been very easy for him to have pressed the Gravity-Defy button on his wrist band, which, together with the Forward-Thrust button would have seen him cover the distance with no exertion whatever. But that would have been cheating. It might also have aroused suspicion from the neighbours. By and large, Basingstoke neighbours are not accustomed to seeing schoolboys floating weightlessly down their streets – except on Saturday nights when they come out of the Golden Lion. Then nothing surprises them. Whole flocks of pink elephants have been known to float aimlessly along the highways and byways. But this was twenty to nine on a Thursday morning, and anything out of the ordinary would certainly have provoked Questions which Kappatoo was very keen to avoid.

So he walked. In the event, it wasn't half as bad as he thought it would be. Once his muscles realized that Kappatoo was serious about walking they resigned themselves to it and stopped complaining. In many ways it was a lot less painful than the school bus, which was extremely old and bumpy. The backs of the seats were adorned with felt-tip messages, like "Kevin-4-Tracey" and "THFC-4-The Cup", and the windows and floor were caked in generations of grime. There was only one face Kappatoo recognized from his historical researches, and that belonged to Belinda Blunt. She was a tall girl with a big nose and jutting-out teeth. At least, most of them jutted out. Some of them jutted in. Over the years, various dentists had tried to get them all to point the same way, and there was more wire holding them together than the wings of a World War One biplane. To make matters worse, she was looking at Kappatoo in a very strange way. He smiled back nervously, which was a bad move. Seeing it as encouragement, she got up from her seat and joined him on his.

"Hello, Simon," she said. He nodded to her, politely, and she jiggled her shoulder against his in a meaningful sort of way, though he wasn't altogether sure what the meaning was. "You don't mind me sitting next to you?" she asked.

Kappatoo shrugged. "No. Should I?"

She seemed surprised and sat for the rest of the journey staring at him and smiling. It made him nervous and he was quite relieved when the bus drew up at the school gates.

"Can I sit with you going home, too?" she asked.

Kappatoo had the feeling he must have missed something when he was researching the twentieth century. Perhaps sitting next to somebody on a bus was all part of an elaborate courtship ritual. Perhaps if he said "yes", poor Simon would have to marry her when he came back. He thought about doing it just for a laugh, but that would have involved sitting next to her wiry smile for another ten minutes, and he didn't need to look forward to *that* after a hard day at school.

"I'll probably walk home," he told her. Such an event seemed about as likely as him crawling up Everest on his hands and knees, but she seemed to accept it. She even seemed resigned to it. She simply said "Oh, all right then," sniffed and turned away sadly.

Kappatoo grimaced and walked across the

playground. The fresh air and exercise, far from making him ill, actually made him feel good! By the time he reached the classroom he felt better than he had at any time since the third of July two thousand two hundred and fifty six, which was when he was born.

Steve Williams greeted him at the classroom door.

"Hey, Simon, did you watch it last night? Wasn't it brilliant?"

Steve was Simon's best friend. Next to Simon's family, he was the person who saw him the most, so Kappatoo had to be very careful. Unfortunately, he hadn't a clue what Steve was talking about.

"Eh?" he said, puzzled.

"The match!" Steve went on. "What a cracking penalty. Bang! Molliof never stood a chance. Mind you, the way Cortsoff took Benson's legs away – that was a professional foul if ever I saw one . . ." Kappatoo didn't know how to answer. Steve was making less sense than Simon's cat. What on earth was a "professional foul"? But he had to say something, and he had to say it quick.

"Yeah," he bluffed. "Fancy getting paid for a foul like that."

Now it was Steve's turn to look puzzled. "Come again?"

"Of course," Kappatoo went on, beginning to panic, "you never actually saw what he did with Benson's legs when he took them away."

"You all right?" Steve asked, concerned. Kappatoo grinned, nervously.

"Yes, um . . . look, I gotta talk to Tracey," he said and hurriedly moved away. Steve watched him go, shaking his head in bewilderment.

Close to, Kappatoo could see exactly why Simon was crazy about Tracey. She was the most beautiful girl he'd ever laid eyes on. Long dark hair, big blue eyes . . . the sort of face that could send a man into unarmed combat with a hundred Droids. Little wonder that Simon, with his limited chat-up abilities, was getting nowhere with her. Kappatoo had spent enough time with *historigrams* of the nineteen eighties to know exactly what to do and say.

"Hi, babe," he began, and slicked back his hair with the heel of his hand. Tracey looked at him, briefly and dismissively.

"Go away, Simon," she told him in a weary voice and looked back at her last night's homework in the exercise book on her desk. Kappatoo wasn't so easily put off.

"Okay, I'll go away. You can come with me.

We'll go away together," he said. "Walk hand in hand by the Lake of Dreams."

She looked up again, a bored expression on her face.

"The Lake of Dreams happens to be on the moon."

"So? We could get a buggy across the Sea of Rains and watch the Earth come up over the Bay of Rainbows. Prettiest sight in all the moon. Whadda you say? Or we could boogie on down the Caves of Apollo and catch a laser show."

It wasn't going like it should. Far from being impressed, Tracey was frowning – much as Steve had done a few moments earlier. "Have you been at your mum's cooking sherry?" she asked.

The romantic approach obviously wasn't working. Not with Tracey, anyway, though it did seem to be having a strange effect on Belinda Blunt who was listening from across the gangway. She had her eyes closed and was clutching her hands together and sighing in a very strange way. Kappatoo decided it was time for a bold, head-on attack. Ignoring Belinda, he gripped Tracey's hand and dropped down onto one knee.

"Tracey, I'm in love," he said, and put on

a very sincere expression. At which point Miss Tweedie, the teacher, came in. She was tall and thin, with lots of sharp corners.

"Simon Cashmere, what on earth do you think you're doing?"

Another voice piped up just behind Kappatoo's back.

"He's talking all sloppy to Tracey Cotton, Miss."

Kappatoo looked round. It was Martin Midgely, the class sneak – a smug-looking boy with carrot-red hair and spots on his chin. Kappatoo stood up.

"In point of fact, Madam," he said grandly, "I'm in love. For Tracey Cotton I would sail the seven seas, perform the Labours of Hercules, conquer Pluto's moon—"

"Yes, well, you can do all that after school. For now we have a lesson to get on with. And for your information, I'm a Miss not a Madam, and Pluto doesn't have a moon."

Kappatoo was indignant. "It jolly well does," he said. "It was discovered in twenty ninety eight by a Brazilian space-probe."

"Sit *down*, Simon," Miss Tweedie said firmly, "and don't answer back." She walked to the rear of the room and back, addressing the whole class. "After lunch we shall have the Computer

Studies exam, and we all know who will come bottom, don't we? Who do *you* think it will be, Martin?"

"Simon Cashmere, Miss."

"Quite. And how do we know that?"

Martin Midgely looked triumphantly at Kappatoo.

"Because he was watching football last night instead of revising, Miss."

"Exactly!" She paused and patted Martin fondly on the head. "And we all know who will come first, don't we?" she went on. Martin glowed and looked more smug than ever. Kappatoo decided he'd just about had enough. Very carefully, so nobody would see, he pressed the Fast-Rewind button on his wrist-band.

"Yltcaxe!" said Miss Tweedie, taking a step backwards.

"SsiM, gnisiver fo daetsni thgin tsal llabtoof gnihc . . ." Martin said, before Kappatoo pressed the Time-Freeze button and the whole class came to a standstill. It looked quite funny, with Martin's mouth open halfway through a back-to-front word and Miss Tweedie leaning over impossibly on one leg. Everyone in the class was frozen in time – except Kappatoo. Very quickly, he got up from his desk and moved across the gangway. At first, he wasn't sure what to do, but then he saw Martin's lunch box. Inside it was a tub of yoghurt. Kappatoo had no idea what it was, but it looked sticky and gooey and just right for what he had in mind. He took the top off and emptied it over Martin's head, then replaced the tub in the lunch box and sat down. Now all he had to do was to press the Time-Restart button and see what happened. Martin Midgely was speaking.

". . . ching football last night instead of revising, Miss."

"Exactly," said Miss Tweedie, and patted him fondly on the head.

"Ugh!" she said, and drew her hand sharply away.

"Ugh!" she said again, and sniffed at it.

"Ugh!" she said for a third time, and then: "Why have you got yoghurt on your head, Martin?"

"Yoghurt, Miss?"

"Black cherry flavour, if I'm not mistaken." It was dripping down his face and the rest of the class was beginning to giggle.

"I don't know, Miss," said Martin, puzzled.

"Well, I suggest you find out," the teacher told him, crossly. "And in the meantime you can get yourself cleaned up."

"Yes, Miss."

He made his way unhappily out of the classroom, cheered on by the other children. Kappatoo smiled to himself. Yes, he thought, the twentieth century *could* be a lot of fun . . .

Chapter Five

Simon Cashmere was having fun, too. Without moving from Kappatoo's room, he had been to the Amazon Rain Forests, sloshed around on the ice at the South Pole and circled the earth in a rocket-ship. But when, for a bit of relaxation, he'd just settled back to watch the opening match of the nineteen ninety world cup soccer finals, the screens and effects suddenly vanished, leaving him staring at blank walls.

"What's going on?" he asked.

"It's nine o'clock," the Computer told him.

"So?"

"Playtime is over. It is time to study."

"You said you weren't interested in what I do."

"I'm not. It's a Citizen's Law. All young persons under the age of eighteen must study for three hours each day between Oneday and Fiveday. Today is Fiveday. Friday, to you."

Simon groaned. He might have guessed there

was a catch to it, and it didn't help to have some invisible computer gloating over him at every opportunity. "Do you have to sound so pleased about it?" he complained.

"Computers can neither be pleased nor displeased," said the Computer, and added: "I'm happy to say."

Simon decided that whoever wrote the program had a sick sense of humour. "So what have I got to study?" he asked.

"You have a choice. History or history."

"That's a choice?"

"You may study the class project or your own personal project."

"What's my project?"

"The twentieth century."

Simon was tempted. At least he knew something about it. Enough, perhaps, to stop the Computer crowing every time he got something wrong. But the twentieth century was boring.

"What's the class project?"

"The Android Rebellion of Twenty One Forty." That sounded more like it!

"Right on," he said, settling back. "Hit me with it."

Nothing happened for a moment – or nothing that Simon could see. Actually the Computer was busily scanning its memory banks to find out what "Right on, hit me with it" meant. The first recorded occasion of the phrase being used was in nineteen sixty-nine when an eighteen-year-old American hooligan called Lee J. Conroy Junior was arrested for setting fire to his neighbour's washing line. When the arresting policeman said "I am going to read you your constitutional rights," he replied: "Right on, hit me with it." The last occasion was in nineteen ninety-two by a boy called Glen Marshall of Littlewick Comprehensive School in Sodbury-under-the-Marsh, Somerset. His teacher had just said to him: "Marshall! What are you doing with that ruler?" and he replied: "Please Miss, Pete Wrighton hit me with it." Between those two occasions, the phrase had been uttered seventeen million nine thousand and forty-seven times in no less than thirty-six countries in the world where English was spoken. In ninety-eight percent of these cases, allowing for regional variations, it meant: "Very well, please do what you suggest." It took the Computer three and a half seconds to collect this information and a further second to conclude that Simon would rather learn about the Android Rebellion than the Twentieth Century. Four and a half seconds was just long enough for Simon to wonder if the Computer had abandoned him, and he was on the point of saying something about it when, with startling suddenness, a giant appeared.

He seemed like a giant, anyway. Not in a Jack-and-the-Beanstalky way because he wasn't an inch over eight feet tall and he probably weighed only a puny twenty-five stone or so. But he was big enough to make Simon jump and shrink away in fear. Then, embarrassed, he realized it was just another hologram and he felt ashamed at being afraid. Just to show him how silly it was he strode up to the giant, punched him squarely on the jaw and nearly broke his fist.

"Ow," he complained.

"I should warn you," the Computer said, "that what you are looking at is not a hologram but a material projection."

Simon didn't have a clue what a "material projection" might be but he certainly didn't want to ask the Computer. There had been more than a hint of amusement in its voice which made Simon think it had fooled him deliberately.

"What you *are* looking at," the Computer went on, "is a real, life-size Android." The real, life-size Android was also looking at Simon. In fact he was looking at Simon far too closely for Simon's comfort. His eyes were a piercing blue, with small, cold pupils which followed his every move.

"Okay," said Simon. "I've seen the Android. Can we go on to something else now?"

The Android took a step forward and the floor shook. Simon gulped, panicked, took a step backwards and fell over his chair. There was a snorting noise from the Computer which sounded suspiciously like a stifled laugh. Simon thought very mean thoughts about it – and the Android took another step forward.

"Androids," the Computer went on, "are very powerful and dangerous." Simon really wanted to know that. "They were built in the years between twenty-one twenty and twenty-one thirty-nine to replace humans as soldiers and policemen." The Android took another step forward and Simon hid behind the central console.

"Look, I've changed my mind," he said. "Perhaps I'm not too interested in the Android Rebellion . . ."

The Computer didn't seem to hear him. "Androids," it went on, "were skilled in all forms of combat, armed with every available weapon of the time, and programmed to be very cunning, evil and bloodthirsty."

The Android paused in mid-step, frowned and spoke. His voice was deep and grinding, like Simon's mother changing gear in her M-reg. Morris Marina.

"And what were *you* programmed for, smarty-pants?" he demanded.

The Computer put on its snootiest voice. "You will please continue the demonstration without comment."

"On yer bike!" growled the Android surprisingly. At least, it surprised the Computer which, once more, had to search its data banks for an unfamiliar phrase. When it spoke again there was an edge to its voice.

"You will continue the demonstration or be sent for metal re-cycling."

This made the Android angry. With an even louder and more terrifying growl he picked up the chair and splintered it in his powerful hands. Simon shrank further back behind the console and began to make all sorts of promises to be good and do the washing-up without complaining if only he could get out of this with all his arms and legs in the right corners.

Somebody must have heard him, because there was a sudden "ploop" and a clatter as pieces of broken chair dropped to the floor. Then there was silence. Simon peered out from behind the console. Then he peered round the other side. Then he stood up and peered over the top of it. The Android had gone.

"Where's he gone?" Simon asked.

"Milton Keynes," said the Computer obscurely. "Please press the Maintenance key on the console." Simon looked for the key and pressed it. The broken chair seemed to dissolve into a pool of liquid. After a moment it re-formed itself into what seemed to be a perfect chair. It was amazing, but just about everything in the future was amazing. Simon waited until it was dry and then sat on it.

"What will happen in Milton Keynes?" he asked.

"Not a lot," replied the Computer. "Nothing ever has."

"So why has the Android gone there?"

"To be melted down."

As scared as he had been, Simon almost felt sorry. At least the Android was brave enough to tell the snooty Computer what he thought of it.

"As you could see," the Computer went on, "Androids were a Bad Thing. In the year twenty-one forty they joined forces, rebelled, and held the human race in slavery for seven months." Simon was then plunged into a fearfully realistic hologram of the battle, with

Androids stomping about the place breaking things. Bullets came out of their fingers, lasers came out of their eyes, and wild oaths came out of their mouths. The air was thick with smoke and rude words, and Simon could feel the heat of battle, smell the burning buildings, hear the victorious cries as mindless bands of conquering robots vandalized the world. It was like watching Millwall play Leeds on a Saturday afternoon. Nothing the humans could do was enough. The Androids had taken over.

Suddenly the image vanished, and Kappatoo's room reappeared. Simon wiped the perspiration from his forehead. He felt drained. So far he'd encountered a deranged Android and lived through a war – and it was still only twenty past nine in the morning.

"So what happened?"

"Doreen Plumpstead," the Computer told him in a hushed and reverent voice. Simon waited for more. On the face of it, Doreen Plumpstead sounded like a very wishy-washy way of ending the most terrifying war in human history.

"Who was she?" he prompted.

A statue appeared of a woman in a heroic pose. It might have been very inspiring, but she wore an old granny shawl round her shoulders, and spectacles, and her hair in a bun – and looked exactly like Simon's dotty Aunt Gracie. It was difficult to imagine anyone like Aunt Gracie ending the Android Rebellion

"What did *she* do?" Again there was no immediate answer. When the Computer spoke again it was almost with a sigh.

"She invented the Droid Eliminator. A simple but brilliant machine. The product of a mind so pure, so logical, so . . . wonderful." Simon was beginning to feel sick. The Computer was bad enough when it was being sarcastic and gloating. But a Computer in love with Doreen Plumpstead was more than he could cope with. Especially a Doreen Plumpstead who looked like Aunt Gracie.

"She received every known medal," said the Computer, "and became the first Heroine of the Planet Earth. Space probes were named after her and for two generations mothers and fathers all called their daughters Doreen. Victory over the Androids Day was declared a bank holiday for ever, and the Droid Eliminator Simulator became the basis of the greatest knock-out cup the world has ever known, replacing the Olympic Games as the final international sporting contest."

The statue of Doreen disappeared to be

replaced by something that looked very much like a mechanical earth digger.

"What's that?" Simon asked, puzzled.

"That," said the Computer grandly, "is the Droid Eliminator."

Chapter Six

Kappatoo knew all he wanted to know about the Droid Eliminator Knock-Out Cup. It was the only competition there had ever been in which everyone in the whole world took part – everyone, that is, except people whose feet couldn't reach the control pedals. This included most people under the age of ten and some people over the age of ten who hadn't grown very much. *Wurlops* on exchange visits from Alpha Pavonis had been banned from the contest because as well as having two heads and six arms, they also had lots of feet which made Droid Eliminating extremely easy for them. *Wurlops* were probably the untidiest-looking creatures in the whole universe. Nobody liked them very much at the best of times, and when a travelling *Wurlop* won the World Droid Elimination Cup and the Doreen Plumpstead Memorial Prize in the year twenty-two forty-one, the Elimination Committee changed the rules so that only proper Earth People could enter. Nobody regretted this, though Kappatoo would have been more than happy to let a *Wurlop* take *his* place. Or even a Dripping *Gluid*. So far as he was concerned, playing the Droid Eliminator was about as much fun as wrestling with an octopus and every bit as tiring. You had to kick pedals, turn wheels, push levers and really concentrate on what you were doing. Kappatoo was usually exhausted after two minutes, and that was just reading the rules.

Half the people in the world were knocked out in Round One. This included nearly everyone over the age of a hundred. Kappatoo's opponent had been an extremely old lady from Papua New Guinea who had actually *fought* in the Android Rebellion a hundred and thirty years before. He beat her by telling her a joke halfway through the Attack Phase and she laughed so much she let a Simulated Android sneak through her defences. His Second Round draw was against a Mexican boy only two years older than himself. Kappatoo bribed him to lose by offering him three weeks' pocket-credits and a life-size hologram of Alpha Juliet, whose song: *I Don't Need No Asteroid Belt To Hold My Pants Up, Baby* was number one in the charts. The Third Round was almost as easy. Kappatoo's opponent, a spaceship mechanic from New Delhi, was called away urgently to repair a Star-Cruiser which had broken down just outside Venus, and he had to forfeit the game. But in the Fourth Round, Kappatoo was struck by a really cruel stroke of Fate.

There were over eighty billion people from a hundred and ninety-six countries left in the competition. The chances of Kappatoo being drawn against another English boy were remote enough, and the odds against him playing somebody from Basingstoke were impossibly high. To be drawn against Sigmasix was about the dirtiest trick Fate could have played on him.

Everyone knew the Sigma family. Sigmasix's elder brother, Sigmafour, had actually got through to the World Quarter Finals the year before and was really famous. With the prize-credits he won, his family had bought the biggest Dome in Basingstoke, and Sigmasix had been sent to the planet Ludilyle for special training. Four months in the unusual atmosphere there had improved his stamina and technique, and, it was reported, he had bopped two hundred and fifty-six Androids in a training session. This was four bops more than his brother had ever managed and only thirty-two bops short of a world record. Not surprisingly, the Sigma family were extremely pleased with themselves and were always bragging about how good they were. This made them very unpopular. Even the travelling *Wurlop* was careful not to boast when he won. After the Victor's Crown had been balanced carefully between its two heads and the sash tied across its various chests, it had shrugged modestly, looked up from beneath twenty-four lowered eyebrows and said:

"Thank you. I don't deserve such an honour." At least, that's how the *Mindword* reported it. *Wurlops* have hundreds of tongues and what it actually said sounded more like a Welsh Male Voice Choir arguing over who should have the last bun at a tea party.

So everyone in Basingstoke really wanted Kappatoo to win – even the Mayor, who wasn't expected to take sides so much as waffle on about what a great honour it was for the town to have two local lads competing together. Sneakily, the Mayor hoped Sigmasix would fall off his ego and break a leg. But while everyone was on Kappatoo's side, nobody – not even his mother – held out any hope at all that he could win. In fact *especially* not his mother.

"Beat Sigmasix?" she would say with a mocking laugh. "You couldn't even beat an egg." She said a lot of things that didn't make sense. Even if an egg had the intelligence to use a Droid Eliminator it certainly couldn't reach the pedals, but it was the tone of her voice which goaded Kappatoo to look for an Answer. This was difficult because he didn't know what the Question was. At first, "How can I beat Sigmasix?" seemed to be a good Question, but there was only one Answer to that: "I can't." Then "How can I cheat?" occurred to him. But while cheating was easy enough in the first three rounds, it was almost impossible after that because there were referees and all kinds of clever gadgets to make sure that everyone stuck to the rules. The Answer, when it arrived, came from the last place Kappatoo ever thought of looking.

His special history project, the Twentieth Century, was every bit as boring as all the rest of history. True, there were a couple of world wars - but nothing big like the Inter-Galactic battle of the twenty-second century. Whole solar systems had been blown up in that. Or the Android Rebellion. That had been a *proper* war, with lasers and thought-grenades and all the humans on the same side. What did anyone ever do that was so special in the twentieth century? They invented computers and aeroplanes and a few men walked on the moon. Wow! Going to the moon took seven milli-seconds in a *tele-thrust* and there was a regular service every five minutes – at least, that's what the timetable said. Usually you would wait quarter of an hour and three *tele-thrusts* would come along at once. But nobody ever thought going to the moon was a big deal. All in all, Kappatoo wished he'd chosen the twenty-second century when things really started to hum, or even done a different planet altogether, like Porex. Until, that is, he was idly scanning a video-*historigram* and the Olympic Games popped up. *Which* Olympic Games didn't really matter because any one of them would have had Kappatoo staring in total disbelief. He had never seen anything like it in his life. People were running and jumping and, even more frighteningly, swimming – as if they were the most natural things in the world. He'd never seen anything like it. Any one of these people leaping around the stadium could win a Droid Elimination Contest in the dark with their legs folded. That was when the Answer hit Kappatoo full in the face: he would have to find one of those people – someone who looked like him and who he could con into swapping places for a day or two.

"Well?" he'd asked Computer. "What do you think?"

"There are problems," Computer replied. "First, time-travel is illegal—"

"Phooey!" Kappatoo snorted. "That's an inconvenience not a problem."

"Secondly, throughout the history of the Olympic Games, there were only two thousand and six boys of your age who took part. The one who most resembled you was called Wang Ku So." There appeared on screen an image of a small, bewildered-looking Cambodian boy diving off a high board into a pool – which seemed hundreds of metres below. Kappatoo suppressed a shudder and looked closely as the boy emerged apparently unscathed from the water.

"He doesn't look the least bit like me!"

"Precisely, sir. The next problem is that if you were to swap places with him, you would have to do what he does. Otherwise people might get suspicious."

Kappatoo almost laughed. Not because there was anything funny. It was just a nervous reaction to the silliest thing he'd ever heard.

"Then," the Computer went on, "the young gentleman doesn't speak English, and *Mindword* would hardly be appropriate. Also . . ."

"All right, all right," Kappatoo said. "I get the picture. In fact I get the complete hologram.

But can't you see? There must be *some*body in the entire history of the world who looks exactly like me, who could win the Droid Elimination Contest – and who could swap places without me having to dive headlong into a bath."

The Computer was silent for a moment, then an image appeared on the screen of a boy who looked exactly like Kappatoo, but without the Ambience Optimizer. He was dressed in animal skins and looked quite tough, in a primitive sort of way.

"That's him! Brilliant!" said Kappatoo. "Who is he?"

"His name is Og, son of Varg the Very Violent – a warrior of the seventh century." The image continued with young Og hacking off a lump of meat from a deer that was roasting over a blazing fire. Kappatoo gagged when Og put the lump into his mouth and began chewing.

"Ugh!" he exclaimed in horror. "That's gotta be the most disgusting thing I've ever seen. *I* can't do that!"

The image changed again. This time another boy who looked identical to Kappatoo appeared on the screen. He was wearing extremely pretty clothes and had a white, curly wig on his head.

"This is a serving boy in the court of Louis the

Sixteenth of France. He spoke perfect English but had his head chopped off in the Revolution." Kappatoo shook his head.

"Looks a bit of a wally to me. What's that on his head?"

"A wig, sir. Very trendy at the time." Kappatoo thought about it then shook his head again. No way could he have worn all those curls – even if it were only for a few hours.

"Look, Computer," he said. "Let's keep this nice and simple, okay? I want an ordinary boy from the twentieth century, who looks like me and who's fit. I don't want a savage from the seventh century or some girly out of the French Revolution. Just a regular guy, okay? From Basingstoke."

"Basingstoke, sir?" the Computer checked with just the hint of a sneer in his voice. "I'll just scan the data." And that's when Simon Cashmere appeared, playing football with Steve in the park. Kappatoo didn't need to think about it.

"That's him," he said immediately and settled back with a smug grin on his face.

To Kappatoo, the idea was as beautiful as it was simple. Simon Cashmere was fitter and faster than anyone in the future. Much, *much* fitter and faster than Sigmasix. He could win the fourth round easily - and no one would mind too much when Kappatoo lost the fifth round because that would be against someone from Bognor or Bangladesh or far enough away that they wouldn't leap around Basingstoke showing off about it.

Now he was in the twentieth century, Kappatoo was beginning to realize that in his excitement at solving his problem in the future, he'd completely overlooked the problems he would meet in the past. Like playing football, for instance. Simon Cashmere was crazy about football. Simon Cashmere was also very *good* at football, not least because he was a fast runner. Kappatoo had never actually *run* anywhere in his life, and was still trying to adjust to the idea of walking. To make matters worse, he didn't even know the rules. From the distant viewpoint of the twenty-third century, "football" was twenty-two boys running round a field kicking something that hadn't done anything to deserve it. Actually *playing* it would be ten times worse than the Droid Eliminator. And dinner-time brought just that possibility . . .

Kappatoo had followed Tracey Cotton into the

playground, hoping to continue where he left off in the classroom, but Steve Williams was hanging around with a football in his hands and a puzzled expression on his face.

"What are you doing?" he asked.

"Telling Tracey a joke," Kappatoo replied. He'd tried the romantic chat-up, now he was going for laughs. "It's an old joke, but a good joke. All right?"

Tracey looked bored, and continued to walk. "Do you have to?" she asked.

"Yes, listen to this . . ." Kappatoo grabbed Tracey's arm. "And can we stand still for a moment? All this walking'll be the death of me." For a moment, Tracey actually looked concerned.

"Are you ill?"

"No, it's all this physical stuff. I'm not used to it. Anyway, listen to the joke. There was an Englishman, a Scotsman and a *Flenk* from A.C.—"

"What, A.C. Milan?" Steve asked.

Kappatoo sighed. "Alpha Centauri, dumb-head."

"What's a *Flenk*?" Tracey asked.

"A sub-human biocarp." He broke off. It suddenly occurred to him that this joke wasn't going to work.

"What's a biocarp?" Steve asked, and Tracey began walking away.

"No, wait!" Kappatoo called.

"I think you're going mental," she said over her shoulder. "Except you can't, 'cos you're mental already."

Kappatoo hurried after her and came very close to running, which frightened him nearly as much as it surprised him.

"What about football practice?" Steve called.

"I don't want to play football, I want to go with Tracey."

He caught up with her. "I don't know why you bother," she told him. "I don't want you, I don't want to go out with you – in fact I don't want anything to do with you. I've told you a million times. I want a boyfriend who thinks there's more to life than football."

"But I've just given *up* football!" Kappatoo protested.

"Shame, it was the only thing you had going for you." She tossed her head and walked away. Kappatoo stayed where he was, feeling rather silly. Girls in the twentieth century were just as unreasonable as they were in the twenty-third. Obviously some things never changed. Steve had gone too, but Belinda Blunt had appeared and was walking towards him with a gleam in her eye that was even more frightening than the thought of playing football. In a panic, Kappatoo pressed the Fast-Rewind button on his wrist-band and started Time again two minutes previously . . .

"What's a Flenk?" Tracey asked.

"A sub-human *biocarp*." He broke off. It suddenly occurred to him that this joke wasn't going to work.

"What's a *biocarp*?" Steve asked, and Tracey began walking away.

"Do you really want to know?" Kappatoo asked.

"No, I want to get some football practice in – we've got a big match tonight." Tracey had gone and Belinda would be arriving in about a minute and a half. There wasn't time to think up an excuse.

"Well?" Steve prompted, bouncing the ball challengingly.

Kappatoo shrugged, sneakily pulled a small aerial from his wristband and aimed it at the football. "So let's play," he said, and pressed the Molecule Re-Integrator button. The air inside the ball was instantly changed into Gossamex–100, the lightest substance in the universe. Instead of bouncing down onto the playground it floated up and away like a balloon. Steve watched it in disbelief until it was a small speck disappearing into the clouds. Then he turned to look at Kappatoo.

"How did that happen?" he asked.

But Kappatoo had gone . . .

Chapter Seven

Simon Cashmere had never been too sure where babies came from. He'd learnt about it at school, of course, and he'd seen all the diagrams and educational films. It was okay as a theory – like Evolution and How The Universe Began – but it seemed to be awfully unlikely. So he was pleased to discover that Science had come on considerably by the year two two seven zero, and that now there were different theories altogether. After an exhausting and heart-stopping *historigram* about the Android Rebellion, he was treated to a very interesting *biologram* about where babies *really* come from. He actually saw them growing in big glass tanks. They started as a weeny egg and an even weenier sperm which came together with the help of a microscope – and then just grew and grew until they actually *looked* like human beings. He still wasn't sure where the egg and sperm came from in the first place but, Simon guessed, that would come in a later lesson. But once the scientists had done away with all that nonsense about pregnancy and mothers' tummies women began doing all sorts of exciting things, just like the men had always done.

Kappatoo's mother was a deep-sea fisher-person, and she was very good at it. She was personally responsible for catching all the fish in the Dogger and Tyne areas of the North Sea and chasing any stray ones that drifted into Forth and Cromarty. This made her very busy for most of the time, and she rarely came out of her room in the Basingstoke Dome. She had sixteen computers to control which, in turn, controlled a fleet of trawlers and all the weather off the north-east coast of England. Simon was lucky to meet her. Not just because she was an important person, but because she didn't have time to meet people much. As it was, she wandered into Kappatoo's room, smiled in a distant kind of way, said "Hello" and wandered out again. She was exactly the kind of mother Simon had always wished *he* had.

No sooner had she gone than the Computer announced:

"Sigmasix wishes to come in."

Simon glanced at the door, surprised that Kappatoo's mother hadn't mentioned he was there. "So let him in," he said. He didn't particularly want to meet Sigmasix just yet – if at all – but it seemed rude to keep him outside.

The Computer sighed. At least, that's what it sounded like. "You are standing on the *anthro-kinetic* platform."

Simon glanced down. He had no idea what an *anthro-kinetic* platform was. What he was standing on looked suspiciously like the floor.

"Say again?" he said to the Computer. Perhaps he'd missed something.

"If Sigmasix comes in while you're standing on the *anthro-kinetic* platform your bodies will merge into a single unit. This, I suggest, would be undesirable. It would also be unpleasant to look at."

Simon still didn't know what the Computer was talking about, but he shrugged and moved away for the sake of a quiet life. Nothing happened for a moment, then there was a distant hissing noise that came closer and closer and ended with a loud sneeze.

The sneeze actually came from a boy of about Simon's age who had magically appeared where he was standing moments before. He sneezed again so there would be no mistake about it, then looked up.

"Hullo," Simon said politely.

"It's all right," the boy replied. "You don't have to try and creep round me. There's nothing you've got that I want."

Sigmasix made even less sense than the Computer. "In fact," he was saying, "there's nothing you've got that I haven't got myself, only better." He was walking round the room with a superior air, looking at things in the same way Kappatoo had looked at Simon's football boots.

"I don't know what you're talking about," Simon told him.

"Ha!"

It was easy to see why he wasn't at the top of Kappatoo's list of favourite people. Simon had known him less than a minute and he wasn't top of *his* list, either. To be fair, he was sturdier and fitter than other Future People, and might even have been quite good-looking, though Simon couldn't be sure. When somebody looks down their nose at the world you can only see their nostrils.

"We've got our own Vidi-Satellite," Sigmasix went on, meaningfully. It sounded meaningful, anyway, Simon thought. He just didn't know what the meaning was.

"I'm happy for you," he said cautiously.

"Reaches everywhere on the planet. Good,

eh?" He was looking at Simon strangely, as if expecting a reaction. Simon shrugged.

"It means," Sigmasix said, spelling it out, "that I can call up anyone in the world on a vision-link."

Simon's frown must have been close to the reaction the other boy was looking for because he smiled victoriously.

"So I called up Carlos San Pedratwelve," he said. "In Mexico. And guess what! He had a life-size hologram of Alpha Juliet. Now where would he have got that from, I wonder?"

"I've no idea," said Simon honestly.

"Ha!"

Sigmasix seemed to like saying "Ha!". Simon felt he ought to say something.

"What's all this got to do with me?"

"You gave it to him. As a bribe. To lose the last round."

Simon pulled a face. Bribing contestants was just the sort of thing Kappatoo *would* have done.

"So I thought you might like to try bribing me," Sigmasix went on, and burst out laughing. "Can you imagine! The Kappa family having anything *I* would want!"

Simon was angry suddenly. "No, I shan't have to bribe you," he said boldly. "I'm going to beat you fair and square."

Sigmasix laughed even louder. "Tell you what," he said. "I'll give you something to think about. A demonstration . . ." He looked round the room. "How do you summon your computer?"

"You don't *summon* me," said the Computer haughtily. "I'm here already."

Simon had never felt like kissing a computer before, specially this one. Sigmasix was not so impressed.

"Never mind the back-chat," he said. "Just give us a Mark Four Droid Eliminator Simulator and look snappy about it." He glanced across at Simon. "Now you'll see how good I am."

Another mechanical digger appeared in the room, but this one wasn't quite so diggerish. There was a cockpit with a seat and an array of controls, levers, pedals and wheels. It was like a cross between the flight deck of Concorde and the signal box at Basingstoke Station. Except, of course, there weren't any wings and trains and things. It seemed very complicated to Simon, and he began to feel a bit silly saying he would win. He didn't even know how it worked.

Sigmasix had no such problem. He jumped into the cockpit, fastened a safety harness and ran through a quick check of all the instruments and controls. Although he didn't want to be,

Simon was impressed. The other boy seemed to fit the Droid Eliminator as if it had been built around him. Kappatoo must have been *really* bad at it if he expected a complete newcomer to do better. But it was when Sigmasix threw the Start Switch that Simon's heart finally sank and buried itself quaking in his tummy somewhere. The whole room suddenly went dark, except for a spooky glow from inside the Eliminator which, Simon saw, came from a digital read-out above the windscreen and stood at 0-0-0-0. And there was a low, frightening hum which didn't seem to come from anywhere in particular. Then everything was light again, but Kappatoo's room had gone and they were surrounded by burning houses and streets – just like in the Android Rebellion. Simon guessed that none of it was real, but it looked and sounded real and it was just as scary as if it had been. Sigmasix crouched over the controls, his eyes darting about amongst the buildings, his whole body tensed and ready. For several seconds nothing happened – then Sigmasix burst into action, his arms and legs moving frantically. It wasn't until a long, laser-like beam hissed out of the Eliminator that Simon actually saw what Sigmasix had seen. Three Androids were approaching from the fire of one of the houses.

Somehow the flames didn't seem to affect them – but the laser beam did! It struck the first Android squarely in the chest, and the robot machine simply stopped moving then slowly toppled over. Simon noticed the digital read-out clicking onto 0-0-0-1 . . . then quickly onto 0-0-0-3 as the other two Androids met a similar fate. Suddenly there were Androids everywhere, closing in on Sigmasix – but he was more than equal to them and soon his score had moved on to a hundred. Gradually Simon came to see it for what it was – a very complicated video-game – and once his fear had gone he began to take more of an interest in what Sigmasix was doing. He watched to see which levers fired which laser, which pedals turned the Eliminator round, which controls changed the angles and put up defences. He had to admit that Sigmasix was really good at it – until, that is, one of the Androids came close enough to throw a grenade. It didn't seem to explode. Not with a bang, anyway. It simply went "Pouff!", but the effect on Sigmasix was really strange. He frowned, and all his movements became much slower, as if he couldn't remember what he was doing. For several seconds he was firing and missing, his score staying the same. By the time he'd fully recovered the game was almost over.

He managed to eliminate a few more Androids then suddenly the scene of battle vanished, the humming noise stopped and Kappatoo's room returned. Sigmasix glanced up at his score and punched angrily at a lever. His face and chest were drenched with sweat and he was panting.

"A hundred and seventeen! That's terrible!" He glared angrily at Simon and growled:

"What did you do?"

"I didn't do anything."

"Yes you did. You must have! That's my lowest score all year."

Simon shrugged. "Please yourself. Think what you like."

Sigmasix climbed out of the Droid Eliminator then turned back and lashed out a kick at it.

"There's something wrong with it. *You* have a go. Bet you don't get half my score."

This was the moment Simon had been dreading. Somehow he'd imagined a chance would come for him to have a quiet practice on his own. He certainly didn't expect to go straight into it cold, with Sigmasix looking on. He gulped, breathed deeply, and climbed into the machine. It looked even more complicated from the inside. There were gauges, meters, flashing lights, information read-outs, scanners, alarms, firing-buttons . . . and that was before you came onto the actual controls. Simon cast a bewildered eye over them all, hoping that Sigmasix would think he was carrying out a normal check, like he had done. Then, when he could delay it no longer, he sighed to himself and pressed the Start Switch.

The next ten minutes were a total disaster. Even the attacking Androids couldn't understand why they weren't being eliminated. At first they behaved as if Simon was trying to trick them and they were really careful. But once they realized he simply didn't know what he was doing, they attacked in force. Nothing Simon did was right. He pressed all the wrong buttons, pulled all the wrong levers, kicked all the wrong pedals. And it wasn't long before the first grenade hit the Eliminator. It was the strangest feeling! There was no explosion and nothing happened that Simon could see, but his thoughts all became jumbled. He found himself thinking about Tracey Cotton and football – he even thought about Tracey *playing* football, which was *really* silly – and he thought about the cat and his newspaper round. Everything, in fact, except Androids. And then it wore off and he was back in the battle again. But it was too late. After just a few more seconds Kappatoo's room came back and the lights were on again. Simon glanced up at the score read-out. It still showed 0-0-0-0. And Sigmasix was doubled over, laughing and pointing at him.

"Nothing!" he choked. "You actually scored *nothing*. I've never known anyone to score *nothing* before . . ."

Simon climbed out of the Droid Eliminator feeling very stupid. "So I had an off day," he said lamely.

"An *off* day? Even my old granny gets more than that – and she's a hundred and three!" He was jumping up and down in glee.

"You just wait till I tell them at home," he was saying. "They'll never believe it. Nothing!" He was looking eagerly round the room. "Where's your *anthro-kinetic* platform . . . I just can't wait! *Nothing*!"

Simon silently pointed to the bit of floor with a fancy name and Sigmasix stood there, still laughing at him.

"That thought-grenade really did you in. Not that you were scoring much before. In fact you weren't scoring anything." Tears of laughter were now gleaming in his eyes. "All right, Computer," he said, "Send me home. I've just got to tell my father." He shook his head, said "Nothing!" just once more, and vanished.

Simon stood very still for a few moments, smarting under Sigmasix's ridicule. Then he straightened his back, squared his shoulders and said:

"Computer, I want to know everything there is to know about the Droid Eliminator . . ."

Chapter Eight

Tracey Cotton hadn't always been horrible to Simon. In fact up until a few months before he was whisked away to the year 2270 she'd even been friendly with him. Of course, Kappatoo didn't know this but if he'd rehearsed it on his *historigrams* he would have learned the whole story. By a strange coincidence, the whole story began near the North Sea, which was where his mother trawled for fish with a computer . . .

Once upon a time, many, many years before Big Macs and Wimpy Bars had been invented – and even before Colonel Sanders had discovered chickens in Kentucky – Lottie Fairweather was born. She came from a place called Hull, which is somewhere at the top of England on the right hand side. Hull, or "'Ll" as the locals call it, is right beside the North Sea which has always had lots of fish in it. And, being a fishy sort of place, it was only to be expected that

'Ll would have lots of fish and chip shops. One of these, Bert's Fish and Chippy, was run by Herbert Cotton who, by and by, fell in love with Lottie Fairweather. When he married her she became Lottie Cotton, because that's what happens, and they had children because that's what happens too. Albert was the first. He was born in 1939 and the Second World War started almost immediately afterwards though nobody actually blamed him for it. He quickly grew up and learned all there was to know about fish and chips and when he was seventeen he decided to leave home to seek his fortune. And, after scouring the country to find exactly the right place, he came to Basingstoke and started up a brand new business which he called Bert's Fish Bar. This proved very popular, and in next to no time he had fish and chip shops in lots of places as well as having plaice in lots of fish and chip shops.

While all this was happening, Wimpy Bars and Big Macs and Fried Chickens were being invented and there were Chinese restaurants, Pizza Parlours, Spud-U-Likes and all kinds of other exciting takeaways opening up which made Bert's Fish Bars sound a bit boring. So he had to make them look much more trendy and have really fashionable new names like "Piscatorial Pleasures" and "Pisces Paradise".

"The Fishodrome" was the trendiest of them all and actually had a plastic palm tree growing out of the deep frier. Gradually they turned into restaurants and delicatessens with waiters and wine and starters and stuff and Albert Cotton made lots and lots of money.

Meanwhile, deep in the Hampshire countryside, somebody else was being born and growing up and things. In fact lots of people were, but only one was special so far as Albert Cotton was concerned. She was Carol Farmer and she came from Alresford, which the locals call "Orlsf'd", even though the "l" and the "r" are back to front and it doesn't begin with "O". She was born in 1955 so she was a lot younger than Albert but this didn't really matter much except it meant that he became old and stuffy quicker than she did. They fell in love and got married and she became Carol Cotton and had babies because that's what often happens. One was called Tracey and the other Sharon and they all lived in Hollyhock Drive which is ten minutes' walk from Lupin Way where Simon Cashmere lived. By this time, Albert Cotton was extremely rich. This brought lots of problems. For a start, rich people don't do the same things as poor people because if poor people can do them there's no point in being rich. Albert Cotton felt there were certain things his family must and mustn't do. He had to drink wine with his meals even though he preferred to slurp down a pint of good Yorkshire Ale. His wife couldn't go to Bingo and his children couldn't play football. Fortunately his children were both girls who didn't want to play football anyway, but to get the point across he made a rule that his daughters could only go out with boys who played rugger. So far as Simon Cashmere was concerned this was a Very Bad Thing because he not only played football but was captain of the school team and top scorer in the entire league. So when, one day, Tracey invited him for tea she said: "Don't let on to Dad that you play football." Until this moment he had never really noticed Tracey, but now that she was inviting him to tea he suddenly discovered that she was extremely gorgeous. Actually, until this moment he hadn't noticed any girl apart from Belinda Blunt – and only her because she'd entered the trials for school goalkeeper. But now that he'd noticed girls properly there was only one thing to do – and that was to fall head-over-heels in love and to pursue Tracey with the same enthusiasm that he pursued the Hampshire Schools Challenge Cup. He felt a bit rotten having to deny the other love of his life, football, but he agreed and promised not to mention it all evening. If he failed it would ruin everything. As it was he ruined everything by burping at the tea table instead.

Tea was a sort of salad with hardboiled eggs, lots of rabbit food and brown bread with hard chippings in which break your teeth but are really good for your tummy. Simon felt the burp coming for several minutes but there wasn't much he could do about it. He couldn't tell it to go away because it wouldn't have listened, and he was beginning to be afraid even to speak in case the burp sneakily chose to escape as soon as he opened his mouth. He decided there was only one thing to do – and that was to disguise the burp under a cough. But that wasn't how it happened. The burp, when it came, was a much bigger one than he expected – in fact it was so loud nobody even noticed the cough which was supposed to disguise it. And to make matters worse it made his hand jerk down on his fork which became a sort of lever and tossed a hardboiled egg into the air. It didn't go very high – only about six inches – but then it landed in Mr Cotton's glass of wine. Mr Cotton jerked backwards in surprise, forgetting that he'd tucked the bottom of the tablecloth into his collar as a napkin, and Sharon Cotton's plate fell off the other end of the table and landed on Fluffles, the family Doberman, which promptly bit Simon's foot. Tracey went very red with embarrassment, burst into tears and ran out of the room. Mrs Cotton simply said: "Well!" and they all sat round and looked at Simon accusingly.

Tracey didn't speak to Simon for several days after that – and it was several weeks before she'd forgotten the evening enough to consider going to tea with him when he asked her. By this time, the incident had been blown up out of all proportion by her dad and, when telling friends about it, Mr Cotton would describe how Simon threw his plate across the table, knocked the wine on the floor and kicked the dog for good measure. In the meantime he'd also discovered that Simon was school football captain, that his mother drove an M-registered Morris Marina, and they really weren't the sort of family extremely rich people should be mixing with. So when Tracey came home from school one day and said she was going to tea with Simon Cashmere there was an enormous argument.

"You're not going to tea with that boy if it's the last thing you do," bellowed Mr Cotton. "I absolutely forbid you to have owt to do with him." "Owt" is a strange word used by people who come from 'Ll and it means "anything".

"But I've *said* I would now," Tracey argued.

"I don't care about that!"

"But it would be really rude not to—"

"Not half as rude as throwing his dinner at me and kicking Fluffles."

"But they'll have got it all ready—" And so on. Eventually, after lots of shouting, Mrs Cotton, who wasn't quite so old and stuffy, persuaded her husband to let Tracey go. But he insisted that she must wear her very best dress and behave like a complete young lady to show them what well-brought-up children are like.

So Tracey washed her hair, put a ribbon in it and wore her very best dress. This made her look like a well-brought-up young lady. It also made her look like Alice in Wonderland. Then Mr Cotton drove her round to Lupin Way in his shiny red Mercedes and watched as she knocked at the door.

"Yes?" inquired Simon's mum.

"I'm Tracey," said Tracey.

"And what can I do for you, Tracey?" asked Simon's mum looking suspiciously at the Mercedes.

"I've come to tea."

"That's nice. Am *I* invited?"

Tracey looked puzzled. "Simon asked me."

"Did he now?"

Tracey looked even more puzzled . . .

It wasn't Simon's fault that he forgot. It was Steve's father's. He'd managed to get three tickets for the Arsenal match against Southampton and had driven the lads off to the Dell to watch it. In the excitement Simon had simply forgotten about tea and Tracey.

Simon's mum did her best to smooth things over. She went out to Mr Cotton in his Mercedes and tried to explain the misunderstanding. He replied that he'd never been so "yumiliated" in all his born days – a fact that very swiftly changed when his Mercedes failed to start and half of Lupin Way had to rally round and give it a push. After that, Tracey was Very Cross Indeed and Mr Cotton banned her from ever speaking to Simon again. But all that was several months before and she had mellowed a lot. Now, instead of ignoring Simon, she simply treated him like something that had crawled out of a dead fish. So it wasn't really Tracey's fault if she was horrible to Simon. It wasn't Kappatoo's fault, either, though he was beginning to get a complex about it.

Steve Williams found him in the classroom after dinner.

"But where did you *go*?" he asked. Kappatoo shrugged and looked as innocent as he could, which would have scored about three out of ten if he'd been marked for it. Fortunately Steve was more concerned with the football.

"Didn't you *see* it?" he demanded. "It just went up and kept on going up."

Kappatoo looked doubtful. Actually he wasn't doubtful at all, but he was trying to dislodge a tiny piece of school dinner from his tooth and it screwed his face up so it just *looked* doubtful by accident.

"You don't believe me, do you?" Steve said. There were all sorts of things Kappatoo couldn't believe. He couldn't believe he'd actually eaten a school dinner for a start. It was hideous. He couldn't believe he'd *run* across the playground while Steve was gazing up into the sky. He couldn't ever remember running before. It was a very upsetting experience. Especially being out of breath afterwards. Footballs floating off into the Ozone Layer were easy to accept.

"Sure I believe you," he told Steve.

"Well I don't," said Martin Midgely, who had been listening to their conversation. "I think you've lost a school football and made up that story as an excuse." Bits of black cherry yoghurt had congealed in his hair, making it stick up in a spiky way. He looked more like a punk rocker than the Class Sneak. "I bet you kicked it into Mr Toop's garden." Mr Toop was more commonly known as Dracula because he bit people's heads off, had low-fat skimmed blood on his breakfast cereal and worked for the Income Tax people. When parents and school teachers told children not to talk to strange men they always thought of Mr Toop because he was *really* strange. Nobody wanted to talk to him anyway because he only had his teeth in when he was in vampire-mode and consequently spat a lot. His garden backed onto the school field and whole generations of balls had disappeared into it. Footballs, cricket balls, tennis balls, baseballs and rugby balls vanished without trace. Even, it was said, the Annual Basingstoke Carnival Queen Ball had once strayed into Mr Toop's back garden never to be seen again. Moments after a ball went over the fence Mr Toop's wizened old face would appear and crack into a toothless leer of glee. "Ahaaaagh!" he would growl, like Long John Silver, "Oi do 'ave another baaall," and he would roll his eyes in appreciation and drop down behind the fence again. Some people believed he was running a very successful sports shop in the front garden.

"Who kicked what into Mr Toop's garden?"

asked Belinda Blunt. She had spend her entire dinner hour looking everywhere for Simon. Fortunately for Simon she hadn't thought of looking two hundred and eighty years into the future. And Kappatoo, whom she *thought* was Simon, had spent his entire dinner hour hiding from her. Now they were back in the classroom again and there was no escape.

"Nobody kicked anything into Mr Toop's garden," Steve told her.

"But Superman here just kicked a football into Outer Space," Martin Midgely sneered.

"I'll kick your *head* into Outer Space in a minute," Steve retorted, and Kappatoo chose the moment to sneak away and sit next to Tracey. She had been home for dinner and was now getting some books out of her desk. The problem for Kappatoo was that he didn't know what to say. He'd tried being romantic, he'd tried being funny, he'd even told her he'd given up football – which wasn't exactly true, but *she* didn't know that. And nothing seemed to have any effect. So, at a loss for words, he simply looked at her and smiled.

"Yes?" she said. It was only one word, but somehow she managed to make it mean: "What have I done to deserve having a miserable worm like you sitting next to me just when I've had my dinner?" Kappatoo didn't care. Well, he *did* but he was determined not to be put off. He decided to try something completely new. Something he had never tried before. Something he didn't even know how to do properly. He decided to be honest.

"I want you to come out with me," he said. She pretended to yawn.

"I know," she said. "You've told me at least a hundred times a day for the last three months. I shan't say it's boring, but I do get more excitement from listening to the fridge humming."

Kappatoo began to wonder what on earth Simon had done to upset Tracey. Being boring somehow didn't seem bad enough. "So why don't you?" he asked.

"Why don't I what?"

"Come out with me. After school."

She sighed heavily and looked at the ceiling. It was still there, so she looked back again. "And where would you like to take me?" she asked. "To watch you playing football?"

"*I'm* not going to play football," Kappatoo said, horrified.

"Of course you are," she told him. "You've got to. It's against Winchester and you're the star player." She said it as if being the star player was something slightly nastier than being a porcupine in a pillowcase.

"I'd rather take you out," he said. That way he would kill two birds with one stone. Go out with Tracey *and* get out of playing football.

"Not likely," she retorted. "Then everyone would blame me if we lose."

He pulled a face and moved to stand up. Something about his face must have made her feel sorry for him because she touched his arm.

"All right," she said. "I'll make a deal with you. I'll go out with you tomorrow night on three conditions, all right?"

Kappatoo thought about it. Tomorrow he would be back in the future, but he had promised to chat Tracey up for Simon so it wouldn't hurt to go along with it.

"What conditions?" he asked.

"First, we go where I want to go – which is to tea with my grandma." When Herbert Cotton passed on, his son Albert, Tracey's dad, bought Grandma a little cottage in Upton Grey – which is a weeny village in Hampshire where people prepare for the great hereafter by shuffling round the pond and feeding the duck. Grandma Cotton didn't know anybody and even the people she didn't know didn't understand her anyway because she came from 'Ll and used words like "owt". She quickly got bored feeding the duck and prodding at things in the hedge with her stick so she complained to Albert that she wanted to go back to 'Ll because she missed the Bingo. Mr Cotton was horrified and said it was only because she was lonely. So every so often Tracey was sent over to Upton Grey on her bicycle to have tea with Grandma. She didn't mind too much because she thought Grandma was fun and she never complained if someone accidentally burped at teatime or played football for the school.

Kappatoo thought he would rather sit and listen to the fridge humming than go to tea with *any*one's grandma but he didn't say so. "Go on," he said instead.

"The second condition is that if you don't keep the *third* condition, you never ask me out again."

That was an easy one. Kappatoo never *would* ask her out again, but Simon probably would. Trouble was, nobody would appreciate the difference.

"And the third?" he asked, but she shook her head.

"No, you've got to agree to the first two before I say."

Kappatoo looked indignant. "Well, that's a

bit cheaty," he protested. She tossed her head and began to busy herself with her books.

"Suit yourself," she said in a way that also meant: "If you don't want to do it you can go away and never speak to me again – oh, and by the way I've seen better-looking faces peering up out of the bottoms of ponds and I get more interesting conversations from my baby sister's Care-Bear."

"All right," said Kappatoo, "whatever you say."

"You'll agree to the third condition?"

"Yes."

She looked at him for a long moment with a mischievous gleam in her eye. "The third condition is that you get top marks in this afternoon's computer test," she said, and burst into hysterical laughter.

Kappatoo shrugged. "Okay," he agreed.

Long, long ago – long before Julius Caesar, Cliff Richard and all the other famous people had been born – there lived a man called Pythagoras. It was such a long time ago that even his name sounds like a prehistoric animal. This man was very clever. While everyone else was coshing brides over the head and dragging them into caves, and generally hacking each other to pieces with swords and things, Pythagoras was busy inventing Arithmetic. The next really famous man was Archimedes. He is famous because he jumped out of his bath and shouted "Eureka!", which is prehistoric for "I've found it!". But even though he lived many years before Archimedes, Pythagoras was much cleverer because he never lost his soap in the bath in the first place. At the time, his friends all told him that doing sums would never catch on and that throwing rocks at sabre-toothed tigers was much more trendy. Nowadays, of course, *every*body can do sums and it's really unfashionable to throw rocks at sabre-toothed tigers – in fact nobody does it at all.

In much the same way, when computers were being invented, everyone said "How frightfully boring!" and became hippies as a sort of protest. They didn't want micro-chips, they wanted big fat greasy chips with lots of salt and vinegar. By the year two two seven zero, however, everybody in the whole world knew about computers. Instead of doing multiplication and division, they were writing programmes to navigate spaceships into the next galaxy – and even that was old hat and fuddy-duddy because computers were quite capable of programming themselves, thank you very much. So when Kappatoo discovered that the test was simply to write a programme to "demonstrate a sub-routine" he nearly fell about laughing. It was so easy! He could do all that sort of thing when he was four years old. In fact it was so easy that he finished it after twenty minutes and there were still forty minutes of the test to go.

Afterwards, when Miss Tweedie had collected up all the papers, Martin Midgely looked across the classroom with a victorious smile on his face. Kappatoo ignored him. He wanted to talk to Tracey, to ask her what her grandma was like. Simon was sure to want to know if he'd got to have tea with her. But he didn't have time to ask her anything. Steve Williams was standing at his desk.

"We've got to hurry," he said. "The coach goes at half past four."

"Coach?" Kappatoo asked. He didn't even know what a coach was, let along what it had to do with him.

"To Winchester," Steve said. He was beginning to think Simon must have had a bang on the head. He'd been acting dumb all day. Kappatoo remembered what Tracey had said about Winchester, and his heart sank. He was supposed to be the star player in a football match . . .

Chapter Nine

Kappatoo's father was a chef. This didn't mean he worked in a steamy kitchen throwing pancakes at the ceiling and mixing up exotic-looking bits of gubbins in saucepans. Food, in two two seven zero, didn't work like that. All the fish that Kappatoo's mother caught, and all the vegetables that machines grew in the fields, were dried and turned into a powder. This was mixed up and called Food. They did wonder about calling it Desiccated Reconstituted Nourishment, but no one could remember that and it didn't sound very tasty anyway, so they simply stuck with "Food". Food looked a bit like sherbert, but was really good for you because it was full of protein and vitamins and stuff like that. Trouble was, it tasted boring, looked awful and slipped through the prongs of the fork when you tried to eat it. So chefs, with the help of the computers, had to make it taste nice and look pretty. They also had to make some things chewy and other things sucky or crunchy. Ice cream still had to be cold and squelchy and taste like ice cream, even though it usually came in a small, mauve cube. But that didn't work for everything. It was no use having roast beef and Yorkshire pudding that was cold and squelchy and looked like spaghetti – even though it was made of the same basic stuff and came in a small *orange* cube with blue stripes. So Kappatoo's father had an important job and he took it very seriously. But it didn't take him very long, so he had much more time for Kappatoo than his mother did, and would often pop in to see him in the afternoon.

Simon had just finished his fifteenth go on the Droid Eliminator Simulator when Father came in. Unlike Sigmasix, one game hardly warmed him up at all, but after fifteen he felt just like he did after a game of football. Father was horrified.

"What are you doing?" he demanded.

"Practising," Simon told him.

"You can't do that!" Father said, and fussed around him like Aunt Gracie, who really believed that if she didn't fuss around everyone the entire world would fall to bits. "You'll wear yourself out!"

Simon could hardly tell him that twentieth-century teenagers didn't exactly wear themselves out playing video-games. They just got a bit warm.

"And anyway," Father went on. "You should be studying. What will happen when the School Inspector goes through your *Study-gram* data file?" Simon didn't even know what a *Study-gram* data file was, never mind what a School Inspector would make of it – but he *did* know when he was being ticked off.

"I'm sorry," he said, and Father looked at him in alarm. Kappatoo had never said sorry for anything in his life. Perhaps, Father thought, he was growing up. The thought pleased him and he patted Simon affectionately on the shoulder.

"That's all right, son," he said. "You just get on and do some now and I'll leave you to it." When he'd gone, Simon told the Computer to put the Droid Eliminator away, then asked:

"What have I got to study?"

"You have a choice," the Computer told him. "You can either study history or history." For a moment, Simon thought he must have travelled backwards in time again by mistake, because he seemed to have been through this before, but the Computer went on: "Your personal project was abandoned without being finished."

Simon thought about it and shrugged to himself. "Go on, then, I'll finish it," he said, and suddenly found himself back in his classroom in the twentieth century. Except, of course, it was just another *historigram* because he could see himself leaning over Tracey's desk talking to her. It was a very strange feeling to be outside yourself, looking in.

"Simon Cashmere!" Miss Tweedie said, and two Simons jumped at the same time. One in the twentieth century and the other in the year two two seven zero. "What are you doing out of your seat?"

Although this happened nearly three centuries before, Simon remembered it as if it were only yesterday – which it would have been if he hadn't swapped places with Kappatoo.

"I was helping Tracey, Miss," he saw and heard himself say.

The teacher pretended to find this very funny. "Ha ha," she laughed sarcastically. "Simon Cashmere *helping* somebody with Computer Studies? You couldn't help somebody out of their coat. You don't *know* anything about Computer Studies. You know less about Computer Studies than I do about World Cup football – which is exactly nothing. So we'll stick to helping people with what we know about, shall we?"

"Yes, Miss," Simon said.

"Good. And tomorrow we shall have a Computer Studies test, and if you do better than *any*body in the class I shall be most surprised."

Simon in the future was getting bored with this. It had been bad enough first time round. "I know all this stuff, Computer," he said. "Can't we move on a bit?"

"The controls are on the console," the Computer yawned. "Must I do *every*thing?" Simon looked along the console for a likely button. There was a Freeze-Frame, Advance, Reverse, and Fast-Forward lever, and a "subject-aimer" like a small steering wheel which didn't mean anything at all to him. He turned it this way and that and found himself looking at different objects and people in the classroom. It *had* been focused on himself – which was where Kappatoo must have left it – so he returned it to its original position and moved the Fast-Forward lever instead. Everything speeded up into a bewildering blur which made him feel so sick he let go of it again, shut his eyes and clutched at his stomach. When he looked up he found that time had moved on about thirty hours. The classroom had gone and he was watching himself walk out onto a field to play football against Winchester Juniors. The only problem was that he had never played football against Winchester Juniors. Tonight's match was the first time the teams had ever met. It was a semi-final of the Hampshire Schools Challenge Cup – the most important game of the season so far. He'd forgotten all about it. Then he realized with a feeling of despair that it wasn't *him* walking out onto the field – it was Kappatoo. And Kappatoo had never played football before in his life . . .

Kappatoo was disgusted.

"But this is real *grass*!" he was saying. Steve Williams tutted. His friend *was* cracking up. He was sure of it.

"You expect a *plastic* pitch?" he asked. "Against Winchester Juniors?"

"But we can't play on grass," Kappatoo protested. "*Things* live in it. Things with lots of legs. Spiders and other strange life forms."

"So?"

"So it's not very nice, is it? Treading on them? They've got families to go home to. There's Mrs Spider cooking dinner for her husband and he's out getting trodden on by a footballer. Anyway, we'll get squashed bugs all over our shoes."

Steve was getting seriously concerned. Simon Cashmere was their best player. You can't play football if you're worried about treading on bugs. In fact you can't really go anywhere or do anything because bugs are everywhere, even when you can't see them. "It's never bothered you before," he said.

"Hasn't it?" Kappatoo was peering into the grass suspiciously.

"And if they don't get trodden on by you they'll only get trodden on by somebody else."

There was a lot of truth in that.

"Okay," Kappatoo said and shrugged and tried not to think about it. Anyway, there were other things to think about. Like where he was supposed to stand and what he was supposed to do . . .

Simon saw the whole thing on his *historigram*, and it was embarrassing. Kappatoo didn't have a clue. He stumbled around out of position, never saw the ball, fell over a few times and missed at least three easy goals. He looked about as comfortable playing football as an ostrich playing water polo. Within five minutes Winchester had scored twice and all Simon's team-mates were jeering at him. That wouldn't have been too bad, but the trouble was they all thought they were jeering at Simon. What Simon thought was that he would never dare show his face again. Then something happened that was even worse. Kappatoo, who should have been at the other end of the field, was flattened by the Winchester Centre Forward right on the Basingstoke goal line and another goal was scored. The *historigram* showed him crawl painfully to his hands and knees – only to freeze, staring in horror at one of the spectator's ankles. Then he lifted his head. Tracey Cotton was looking down at him with disgust and disappointment. Tracey, who'd said she wasn't coming. Tracey, who had seen all his dismal embarrassment and failure. And Simon, looking back from the future, could do absolutely nothing about it.

"You can't even play football, can you?" he heard her say. "And that's what you're supposed to be best at."

Simon groaned to himself. Far from winning Tracey's approval Kappatoo had made everything a hundred times worse. He should never have listened to him in the first place. He should never have agreed to the Swap . . .

Back in the twentieth century, Kappatoo felt just as embarrassed and humiliated as Simon did in the twenty-third. Something had to be done – and done fast! Very carefully, so no one could see, he pressed the Slow Motion button on his wrist-band. For a fleeting moment, everyone on the pitch became motionless except Kappatoo. He adjusted the control slightly and they all began to move again, but at about a quarter of their normal speed. That was about right, because with Kappatoo moving at his normal speed he was just slightly faster than everyone else . . .

Simon simply didn't understand it. Basingstoke kicked off after letting in their third goal and Kappatoo seemed to have changed completely. Gone was all the falling over and stumbling and being left behind. He became by far the fastest player on the field, tackling furiously, making astonishingly fast runs, dribbling with perfect ball-control and finishing with four goals in as many minutes. Winchester couldn't believe what was happening to them. It was as if Maradona had signed for Basingstoke Juniors. And nobody was more impressed than Simon. Suddenly he began to feel very pleased with himself and he found himself wondering what Tracey thought of it. He turned the subject aimer on the Computer console and looked all round the spectators at the edge of the field. Then he frowned and turned the subject aimer the other way. Then he moved all round the field for a third time and finally zoomed in on the school coach.

Tracey had seen none of Kappatoo's brilliant play. She had gone back to the coach and was sitting inside reading a book.

Chapter Ten

Kappatoo lay back in the bath at Simon's house and thought about the Great Dripping *Gluids*. Perhaps he'd been unfair about them. There was a lot to be said for showers and baths. Specially baths – and *extra* specially after a hard game of football. And it had been a hard game. Although everyone else had been playing at quarter speed, Kappatoo had to pay for the advantage by actually playing four times as long as they did. To them, it was a ninety-minute game. To Kappatoo it had lasted nearly six hours – and for somebody from the future that was a very long time just to be standing up, never mind trotting round a football field. Baths, under those circumstances, weren't too bad at all.

The coach trip home had been brilliant! Beating Winchester Juniors and getting through to the final was something to celebrate – but beating them by thirty-seven goals to three was beyond everyone's expectations. And Kappatoo had scored all thirty-seven goals himself. Of course, everyone thought he was Simon Cashmere, but that didn't matter. He was a hero, and all the rest of the team and the spectators sang "For he's a jolly good fellow" and other strange songs which Kappatoo had never heard before. Even Tracey seemed impressed when she heard about it, though she tried hard not to show it.

"I'm pleased for you," she said, and smiled, which made Kappatoo feel really good.

Simon's mother wasn't so impressed.

"Into the bath!" was the first thing she said.

"But I scored thirty-seven goals against Winchester Juniors!" Kappatoo protested.

"I don't care if you scored a hundred goals against Brazil – you're not sitting at table like that."

Simon's dad was no better. "How did the cricket go?" he asked when, at last, everyone was sitting down to fish fingers and chips.

"I scored thirty-seven goals," Kappatoo told him.

"Hmmm," Dad said. "That's not bad for a bowler." He nodded gravely and turned his attention to the evening paper.

Lucy, Simon's sister, was looking at Kappatoo in a very thoughtful way, as if she knew he wasn't

Simon. Of course, there was no way she *could* have known.

"I know a secret about you," she said suddenly and Kappatoo nearly choked on his fish finger.

"Oh yes?" he said, trying to sound normal. "What secret?"

"Tracey Cotton thinks you've lost your marbles."

Kappatoo sighed with relief. "Why, has she found them?" he asked.

"You know what I mean. She thinks you've gone soft in the head."

"And what would *you* know about it?" Kappatoo asked.

"Her sister's in my class. She told me at dinner time. Said you were talking a lot of rubbish about *Flenks* and *biocarps*. She said you'd lost your marbles and I told her you never had any in the first place."

"Thanks," Kappatoo said, wondering what marbles had to do with it. "As it happens, *Flenks* used to live on Jupiter before they moved out to Alpha Centauri."

Simon's father looked up from his paper. "The Americans are sending a rocket to Jupiter," he said.

"They shouldn't bother," Kappatoo told him. "There's nothing there any more."

"Oh, and you would know, wouldn't you?" said Lucy. "You've been there, of course."

"Had to," Kappatoo shrugged. "School trip. It was dead boring."

"Now, now," said Simon's mother. "There's no need to be sarcastic." And she added for good measure: "Sarcasm is the lowest form of wit," and even Dad looked at her with disbelief. Then the phone rang.

Simon's mother was gone for about three minutes, and when she came back her face was drained of colour and she had to support herself against the sideboard.

"That was Miss Tweedie," she said. "She just had to ring and tell me."

"What?" asked Dad, munching about six chips at once. He didn't dare do that sort of thing unless Mum had gone out of the room.

"It's Simon," she said. "He's got a hundred percent in the Computer Studies exam. Nobody's ever done that before."

Kappatoo shrugged modestly. "Easy-peasy," he said, and added: "Chips are quite nice, aren't they? Can I have some more?"

At that precise moment – well, at that precise moment nearly three hundred years into the future – Simon was actually talking to

Kappatoo's father. Except he wasn't, because he couldn't have squeezed so much as one word in with a hammer and shoe-horn and three pints of axle-grease.

"Now you know what you've got to do, don't you?" Father was asking.

"Yes . . ." Simon began to say, but only managed to get as far as "Y . . ." before Father went on again.

"Take it steady at first. Don't wear yourself out in the first few minutes. *Look* for the Androids before you start firing and don't let them get close enough to throw their thought-grenades."

Simon nodded. "Father, you've told me this about twenty times already," he began to say, but only got as far as "F . . ." before Father went on again.

"And whatever you do, *don't* let Sigmasix put you off. He'll try anything to distract your attention."

"No, Father," Simon actually managed to say.

"Good," Father said, and straightened the shoulders of Simon's brand-new, Droid-Eliminating Combat Leotard. "So we're all ready, are we?" Simon took a deep breath and nodded. This was the big moment. The fourth round of the world contest

"Well. Good luck then, son," Father said and moved across to the Computer console where he pressed a combination of buttons before standing back and giving Simon an encouraging wave.

Nothing he had seen in the future could have prepared Simon for what happened next. Kappatoo's room disappeared and he seemed to be standing in a vast stadium under dazzling spotlights. Thousands and thousands of people were seated all round, and when they saw him a huge cheer went up. To Simon it felt just like he imagined it would feel to run out onto the pitch at Wembley for an F. A. Cup Final. It was great! He turned and waved at the crowd and the cheers grew even louder. Then he saw the Droid Eliminator, crouching in the middle of the arena like an enormous, gleaming spider. For just a moment he panicked, wondering if he would remember what he had learnt during the afternoon. None of his scores had come even close to the best Sigmasix had done, but at least he wouldn't embarrass himself. He was glad he'd spent the time practising . . .

Another cheer went up from the crowd. It wasn't quite so loud as before, but he waved back anyway – until a voice spoke behind him.

"They're not cheering for you, dummy, they're cheering for me."

Simon spun round. Sigmasix was standing there in a shining and very flashy silver Combat Leotard. Even his Ambience Optimizer had been decorated with glinting bits and gold stars. He looked at Simon in a very superior and snooty sort of way for a few seconds and then fell about laughing helplessly.

"Nothing!" he gasped. "I'd never seen it before. You actually scored *nothing*!"

Simon groaned. Did he have to go through all this again? Hadn't it been enough before? Sigmasix strove hard to control himself, his face twisted up as he tried to stop himself laughing.

"Great Dripping Gluids!" he said, wiping tears from his eyes. "*Nothing*!"

Simon very nearly said that "nothing" wasn't such a bad score for somebody who'd never even *seen* a Droid Eliminator before that morning, but fortunately the crowd chose that moment to burst into a vigorous fit of booing. The referee had arrived.

He was tall and very thin, like Kappatoo's father, and wore a long cape. He must also have been wearing some kind of microphone because when he spoke his voice boomed out so that everyone in the stadium could hear.

"Ladies, gentlemen and visiting life-forms," he began, "welcome to the fourth round of the World Droid Elimination Knock-Out Cup in which we shall be meeting, first – and favourite to win – Sigma Six Eight Two Four Four Zero . . . Let's hear it for Sigmasix!"

A few people around the stadium clapped – probably people from the Sigma family, Simon guessed, and then the referee continued:

"And, the underdog, ladies and gentlemen and visiting life-forms, Kappa Two Seven Zero Nine Three Four. Put your hands together please – for . . . Kappatoo!" Almost everyone in the audience stood up and shouted and cheered and stamped their feet. It was embarrassing and Simon almost felt sorry for Sigmasix because nobody wanted him to win – even though they knew he would. Then Sigmasix said:

"Shame all those wallies are going to be disappointed, isn't it?" and Simon didn't feel sorry any more. He just wished there was some way he could do really well to stop his opponent being so big-headed.

The referee took a small gadget from his pocket and pressed one of its many buttons. Future People were very fond of gadgets. This was a Random Start Indicator and was supposed to be a very fair way of deciding who would be first to go on the Droid Eliminator. Simon secretly thought tossing a coin was just as good, but that Future People were probably too lazy to bend down and pick the coin up afterwards. The Random Start Indicator hummed and buzzed for several seconds, then it whirred and ticked and finally a green light came on and it said: "Sigma Six Eight Two Four Four Zero will commence," and the crowd cheered wildly. The referee took another gadget from his cape. This looked like a smaller version of those metal detectors people walk along the beach with, hoping to find coins, watches, silver-plate and other family heirlooms which unfortunate holiday-makers have lost in the sand. This gadget was called a Concealed Advantage Revealer. The referee pointed it at Sigmasix to make sure that he wasn't carrying any cunning gadgets of his own that would help him to cheat. Of course, Sigmasix wasn't, because he didn't need to. He was, after all, playing the only person he'd ever known to achieve the unbelievable score of *nothing*. He lifted his arms, turned round and, when the referee announced that he was given leave to start, walked across to the Droid Eliminator. An excited murmur ran through the crowd as he climbed inside and the lights began to dim.

Then there was silence as Sigmasix pressed the start button.

The vast stadium suddenly seemed to change. It was just an illusion because the crowd was still there, but all everyone could see was the now familiar scene of the Android Rebellion – only this time it was on a much bigger scale. The burning buildings were bigger, the smell of the smoke was stronger and noises of battle all seemed much closer. Then Sigmasix fired his first laser – probably before anyone in the stadium had even seen the advancing Android. Although he didn't want to be, Simon was very impressed. Sigmasix was certainly a worthy favourite, and it didn't surprise Simon at all that he had come within thirty-two bops of the world record – even if it had only been in a training session. The Droid Eliminator hummed and spun, firing in all directions with a deadly accuracy. Androids were falling everywhere – none of them even beginning to get close enough to throw their numbing thought-grenades. And all the while the score read-out was ticking up "kills" at an alarming rate. Then, as before, it was suddenly over and the floodlights came on again. Sigmasix climbed wearily from the Eliminator and stood exhausted and triumphant. The crowd was silent, stunned by his brilliant display.

They had never seen such speed and power before – except, perhaps, on Vidi-Grams of the finals themselves. The referee consulted the read-out, checked it against his own instruments and called the crowd to attention.

"The score for Sigma Six Eight Two Four Four Zero is, ladies and gentlemen and visiting life-forms, an incredible two hundred and sixty-two – the highest ever recorded at this stage of the competition!"

Despite what the crowd thought of Sigmasix, they had to acknowledge what an achievement this was, and everyone stood and cheered. Sigmasix glowed as he strolled back to where Simon stood – and Simon knew he was going to gloat. He wasn't wrong.

"Embarrassing for you, eh?" Sigmasix said. "The crowd might as well go home. There's nothing to see now." Then he began to laugh again. "Nothing to see! Nothing, get it? That's what they're gonna see. Nothing!"

Simon felt very cold and angry – and determined that he was going to score at least a hundred just to show him. After the referee had announced him and scanned him with the Concealed Advantage Revealer he walked to the Droid Eliminator. The crowd seemed to know he could never hope to get an amazing score and they were all silent, feeling sorry for him. The only sound he could hear was Sigmasix, still laughing and saying "Nothing!" over and over again.

The Droid Eliminator was a super version of the one he had practised on. Simon sat inside, checked the instruments and made himself comfortable. He closed his eyes for a few seconds, breathing deeply – just like he did before kicking off in an important football match – then he said a little prayer, tensed himself and pressed the start button.

The battle was like none of the others. For some reason he didn't understand, he could see further, notice things quicker and react much faster than he had in practice. But there wasn't time to wonder about it. There were far more Androids to contend with, and they came at him from just about everywhere – even popping up out of holes in the ground just a few yards away. Within a few seconds he was soaking with sweat and his arms and legs were aching furiously. Very quickly he lost count of how many of the enemy his lasers had hit or how much more time he'd got. He glanced up at the read-out and was completely astonished to see that he had actually bopped no less than two hundred and forty-nine! That was nearly as many as Sigmasix's previous record. Could it be true? He glanced up at the read-out again, just to make sure – and that was a big mistake. A huge Android chose that moment to make a run across the street behind him and lob a thought-grenade. Simon saw him just in time to get in a burst with a laser - and his score clicked up to two hundred and fifty. Then everything went hazy, and his concentration seemed to disappear. All he could think of was Tracey Cotton and Computer Studies, Miss Tweedie and Martin Midgeley. It was as if the Android Rebellion had never happened and he was sitting at home in front of the television. He shut his eyes for a moment and tried hard, *really* hard, to concentrate, and when he opened them again there were three Androids about to clamber onto the Eliminator. He kicked down on the Defensive Shield pedal and spun the laser-bursters in a wide arc above him. The three Androids dropped to the ground and the read-out clicked on a further three points. Again his mind became hazy and woolly. It was a real struggle to think at all, never mind think about what he was doing. All his actions were now happening on their own. He could sense that he was firing and turning and spinning and kicking levers and thrusting out defensive shields, but in his mind he was arguing with his mother, having weird conversations with the cat, holding Tracey's hand . . . And then, suddenly, it was all over. His mind cleared, the floodlights came on and the Droid Eliminator's humming died away. He unstrapped himself and staggered away from it. He had never felt so utterly tired – not even after last year's cup match against Reading Juniors, when his team were down to nine men and they had to go to extra time. The crowd was silent and Sigmasix was frowning in disbelief. The referee consulted the read-out, checked it against his own instruments, then checked both again.

"Ladies and gentlemen and visiting life-forms," he began. "Kappa Two Seven Zero Nine Three Four has scored an incredible two hundred and sixty-four bops . . ." His voice was drowned as the crowd screamed and cheered in delight. Sigmasix glowered at him and walked away without a word.

"This," went on the referee just as soon as he could be heard, "includes an amazing *fifteen* bops scored *after* a successful attack with a thought-grenade. This is three bops more than the world record set up by Zeta Nine Nine Two Four Six Two in last year's final." The crowd cheered and yelled again and then began chanting *Kappa . . . too*, *Kappa . . . too*, and Simon, happy and exhausted, felt his knees buckle and collapsed smiling, onto the floor of the stadium.

Chapter Eleven

Kappatoo yawned, stretched, and looked at the time-piece on his wrist-band. By now, in the year two two seven zero, he knew that Simon would have completed the fourth round of the World Droid Elimination Knock-Out Cup, that the celebrations would all be over and he would be alone in his room waiting to swap back. Lucy had gone to bed, and Mum and Dad had popped out to visit a friend – who just happened to be a barman in the Red Lion, but that was by the way. Kappatoo had waited till Lucy was fast asleep, fallen asleep briefly himself while watching a strange television programme about a man with two hearts who leapt about the universe in an old police telephone box, and thought that there couldn't be a better time than now to give Simon a call in the Future. He stood up, his legs still very stiff from scoring thirty-seven goals, and began to dismantle the telephone.

Simon wasn't alone, as it happened. After his record-breaking win all kinds of people had popped in to see him, suddenly appearing on the *anthro-kinetic* platform after being duly announced by the Computer. His present visitor was even more welcome than the others had been, and when the telephone sounded he was upset to say the least.

"Who is it, Computer?" he asked.

"I shall inquire," the Computer told him, and was silent for a moment before coming back with: "The caller says his name is Simon Cashmere." Simon groaned.

"Can you put him up on a screen or something?" he asked. The last thing he wanted just now was to visit his own living room in the twentieth century.

Kappatoo appeared on a screen, and Simon's visitor gasped at how alike the two boys were.

"About time," Kappatoo complained. "What's the hold-up?"

"I've got a visitor," Simon told him. "How did you make out on the Computer Studies test?"

"Sinchy hundred percent. I also scored thirty-seven goals against Winchester. How did you get on against Sigmasix?"

"Sinchy two hundred and sixty-two bops and a world thought-grenade record."

Kappatoo looked really pleased. "Brilliant!" he said. "So. When are you coming back?"

Simon looked at his visitor, who had long since given up trying to understand the conversation. "I'm in no hurry," he said. "In fact I rather like it here. It's fun being a hero."

Kappatoo's face registered the panic he suddenly felt. "What are you *talking* about? You've *gotta* come back. You can't live there without a wrist-band, for a start!"

Simon looked at his new wrist-band. "I've got one. Told them I lost the other one and they whacked out a new one on the *dupli-transformer*. Everyone's so pleased with me I shan't even have to pay for it. I'm staying on for the fifth round. Might even get through to the finals. Good, eh?"

Kappatoo swallowed hard. "But what about Tracey? I've fixed up a date with her for tomorrow night."

Simon shrugged. "I've got a date for tomorrow night, thanks."

"Who with?"

Simon smiled at his visitor. "Alpha Juliet. She's taking me along as a guest at her concert."

Kappatoo's mouth dropped open in disbelief. "Alpha Juliet? The pop star?"

Alpha Juliet spoke for the first time. "That's

right, Simon, whoever you are. Anyway, darling, we're awfully busy right now. Can you call some other time?"

Back in the twentieth century, Kappatoo found himself cut off again. He looked at the re-built telephone in horror, wondering what he could do, stranded in the past. It was awful! There was nothing he *could* do – Simon had the time-belt with him in two two seven zero! In a daze, he put the telephone back together again and sat staring at it. Gradually it occurred to him that his day hadn't *really* been too bad. He'd come top in a Computer Studies test, had fun with Martin Midgely *and* scored thirty-seven goals in an important football match. He was just as much a hero as Simon was . . . and there was still plenty more fun he could have. He laughed to himself, thinking about it, then glanced through the telephone directory, found her number and dialled Tracey Cotton . . .

ARMADA

All these books are available at your local bookshop or newsagent, or can be ordered from the publisher. To order direct from the publishers just tick the title you want and fill in the form below:

Name ____

Address ____

____

Send to: Collins Childrens Cash Sales
PO Box 11
Falmouth
Cornwall
TR10 9EN

Please enclose a cheque or postal order or debit my Visa/ Access –

Credit card no:

Expiry date:

Signature:

– to the value of the cover price plus:

UK: 60p for the first book, 25p for the second book, plus 15p per copy for each additional book ordered to a maximum charge of £1.90.

BFPO: 60p for the first book, 25p for the second book plus 15p per copy for the next 7 books, thereafter 9p per book.

Overseas and Eire: £1.25 for the first book, 75p for the second book. Thereafter 28p per book.

Armada reserve the right to show new retail prices on covers which may differ from those previously advertised in the text or elswhere.